THE war had been going on for some time.

Every day brought news of a great battle with victory for both sides, which, as all will admit, is an entirely new phase of the oldest art in the world.

The Emperor of Russia sat in his ivory car, and encouraged his soldiers. The Sultan of Turkey could be seen in the distance, bivouacking on pipes and coffee, inferiors in rank being only permitted pipes and tabors.

Fiercely went on the fighting for several hours, with slight intervals for refreshment, and when time was called for the day victory was once again claimed by both.

The night expired, and many soldiers both Turkish and Russian followed suit, but again the position was unchanged, and again both claimed to have won. It was the first time in the history of sport that a dead-heat had been so appropriately discovered.

The Emperor of Russia got out of his ivory car, and placed his fevered hand upon his erewhile placid brow. " What will they say in England ? " murmured he, and an echoing breeze seemed to him to catch up the words and whisper, " What indeed ! "

The Sultan of Turkey laid down his pipe, and swore at his principal backer. " What is the good of my winning while yonder Tartar horde knows not that it has been defeated ? " The backer backed out of the Imperial presence, and the only answer that even the Sultan could obtain was the same as that vouchsafed the Cæsar, " What indeed ! "

A truce was called and a consultation held that very evening, and it was decided—first, that no London daily paper should be admitted into either camp, as it was chiefly through them that both sides believed they never could be beaten ; and second, that an Umpire should be properly appointed to decide who had won and who lost on all future occasions. These resolutions having been properly proposed by the Emperor, and seconded by the Sultan, were put to the meeting, and everyone signified "the same" in the usual way. A cold collation followed, after which and the recognised loyal and patriotic toasts the war proceedings were resumed de novo.

Just then a fresh arrival appeared on the scene, and all knew that a change was at hand. The new-comer was a mild and pensive gentleman, clad in a picturesque garb, and his visiting card bore on it the famous address : " No. 153, Fleet-street, London, E.C." There was a lurking devil in his deep blue eye, and his bullets were made of lead. He was at once, by acclamation and the Imperial ukase specially prepared for this ukasion, appointed sole Umpire, his decision to be final and free from any appeal to a court of law whatsoever.

In the dead watches of the night he was known to be hard at work solving the knotty problem. When morning dawned the halo of joy and peace which illumined his happy face was a thing to see. " I have hit on an expedient," he whispered to the rivals, " and War shall be no more. You see yon target and this gun "—producing both from his waistcoat-pocket, and proceeding to place the former in position— " you see them both ? No one can hit that target with this gun while he is in the wrong. You shall both fire at it, and he who has right on his side will be at once victorious, while he who is wrong will be utterly confounded. Thus will Peace again reign triumphant on earth, and the reign of Wretchedness be over.—Tum-tum."

Even as he spoke a blessed balm seemed to suffuse the air, the sun burst forth from a bank of clouds where it had been deposited, the birds began to sing, the rivers ran babbling as of peace and plenty, and all nature smiled when it was seen that the target of truth and virtue, of wisdom and of wit, was none other than

The Twenty-fifth Volume of the Second Series of Fun.

© 2007 McSweeney's Quarterly Concern, San Francisco, California. This page taken from the frontispiece of *Fun* Vol. 25, from 1877. *Fun* was one of Victorian London's weekly satirical magazines, sort of a livelier and more politically liberal rival to *Punch*. Its last issue appeared in 1901. INTERNS & VOLUNTEERS: Chris Lindgren, Peter Rednour, Ally-Jane Grossan, Annie Wyman, Elizabeth Baird, Nick Buttrick, Jennifer King, Lucy Sun, Jesse Nathan, Alyssa Varner, Gwendolyn Roberts, Flynn Berry, Kristopher Doyle, Claire Powell, Teresa Maria Cotsirilos. ALSO HELPING: Alvaro Villanueva, Andrew Leland, Chris Ying. COPY EDITORS: Caitlin Van Dusen, Oriana Leckert. EDITORS-AT-LARGE: Gabe Hudson, Lawrence Weschler, Sean Wilsey. WEBSITE: John Warner w/ Ed Page and Chris Monks. AMANUENSES: Michelle Quint, Greg Larson. KEY GRIP: Adam Krefman. OUTREACH: Angela Petrella. CIRCULATION: Heidi Meredith. PRESIDENT: Barb Bersche. MANAGING EDITOR: Jordan Bass. PUBLISHER: Eli Horowitz. EDITOR: Dave Eggers. COVER ILLUSTRATION: Leah Hayes. INTERIOR ILLUSTRATIONS: Amy Jean Porter.

Belgian Warmblood

YURI
CONNOR KILPATRICK

A FTER WE GOT BACK from Thanksgiving, management fired three adjustors and hired Yuri to replace them all. Anders, who had not received the phone call, showed up on Monday and found Yuri at his station. Yuri sent him back out into the world with a handshake, a styrofoam cup of coffee, and a highlighted copy of the classifieds in his back pocket.

Yuri was a Yugoslavian bronze-medalist wrestler, which didn't impress me as much as you'd think. Jobs like mine were full of jocks with irreparable tendons, defrocked minor-leaguers in rehab, guys who lost their scholarships and gained seventy pounds in the off-season; bad backs all around. Even fat-ass, screw-lipped Bo supposedly had a Super Bowl ring back from when he was in the pros. But I never saw it. This one time I got up the courage to ask him why, if he had it, he never wore it. "Can't," he said. "Bitch took it."

I worked with Yuri in an old stationery warehouse just outside Dallas and spent most of my afternoons trying to decide how I got there. I had always seen myself as more of a big-picture thinker, a delegator; the valued strategist who'd zero in on some hidden inefficiency and turn it all around like I had just invented coagulation. But there I was, in a giant metal shack with a dirty concrete floor that would smash you into soup if you fell. Big stacks of boxes and pallets like brown skyscrapers reaching toward the distant cosmos of the cobwebbed ceiling. I'd find nests up there, wreathlike constructions big enough for pterodactyl eggs. Sometimes there were bats. I'd get home and be covered in this black warehouse dust so I'd lie down on the linoleum and let my dogs run up and lick it off which I liked because it made me feel like Jesus.

On Yuri's second day I ran a forklift halfway off the dock. I was a little stoned and something in my head slipped. The croak-voiced trucker who was guiding me into his rig said *Whoah! Goddamn!* and jumped clear. I tried to tow it away with another forklift but the latch snapped and the chain flew back past three petrified shipping clerks and tore open two cartons of our most expensive stationery (Crane's Crest 100 percent cotton rag). My boss's head popped up in his office window. Everyone ran over to examine the damage. I slipped away and hid out on the toilet.

I sat and listened to the shouting, the squeaking gears, the crack and fizzle of a caustic voice on the intercom and then more shouting. I found a dirty cartoon folded up in a bow-hunting magazine. I laid it on my thigh and gave my cock a few tugs but gave up and walked out onto the main floor, half hoping they'd all forgotten about my involvement.

But Yuri was there with the croak-voiced trucker. There were many others. Even the Vietnamese machinists had wandered over all the way from the east dock just to watch my crew yank on a pulley threaded through the beached forklift. In a place like that, incompetence is a puff of blood in shark-infested waters.

Yuri said my name and everyone looked at me. The croak-voiced trucker spat a brown curd off the dock.

"Look: the metal. It is weak," said Yuri. Everyone moved in a little closer. He had fashioned a bracket and a hook using scrap metal from one of the shitcanned sorters and sealed it with one of the presses like some ancient gnostic forging. It worked. He towed the forklift off the edge of the dock and more than a few people clapped. "Fucking *finally*," someone said.

Yuri waved them off and took my hand. "I am Yuri."

"I know."

"Jesus H." My boss tapped me on the back. "Operator's license," he said. I handed it to him. He squinted at it, then used the laminated corner to clean out his thumbnail. He tapped both of my sneakers with his boots. Gary was an Army reservist who'd gotten back from the Middle East a few months ago. Over there he'd worked in the dining room of a palace and eaten steak three nights a week. He had the pictures to prove it. Now it was back to a water-stained ceiling and puke-colored carpeting. "Fuck's sake," he said. "Hard-toe. Steel-toe. Not your fucking Nikes."

"Yessir."

"Not your fucking sandals."

"Yessir."

"I'm writing you up."

"Yessir."

"Now get back on that fucking truck."

"Yessir."

The crowd dispersed and I got back on my truck.

Ten minutes later Yuri ran up and grabbed hold of my fork-lift like it was a trolley. I kept driving and made a sharp right but he didn't fall off. Instead he put a hand on my sweaty back and motioned with his chin at the croak-voiced trucker shouting into a pay phone on the dock. "He is a drunk," he said.

"Yeah. So what?"

"He is to blame."

That afternoon I watched as Yuri made his rounds, pouring various oils and polymers down narrow pipes, filing down blades, writing up reports on his clipboard. He monitored five stations at once like he was running a day care. He mopped up any spills with loving strokes and swirls, working swiftly and efficiently with a kind of brutish grace. After a while the Vietnamese crew brought him a bowl of noodles from their steam-clogged break room, which I had always been afraid to visit. I could smell the broth from across the dock: onions and spearmint leaves. Yuri sat where they'd stopped him and bent over the bowl, the white vapors swarming up over his face, a tiny spoon in his fist, noodles streaming from his pursed lips.

Before my shift was over I used my razor to slice open a carton of stationery and spent about an hour writing my initials in the top corner of each page. On the last page I drew an elaborate anatomical cross-section of a whale, complete with organs and bones that did not exist. I added a speech bubble. It said, "Hast thou forsaken me?" It was my tenth month on the job.

On Monday my boss had me unload the gutted carcass of a wild pig from his pickup. Yuri and him had gone hunting over the weekend and the pig was a gift for the Vietnamese crew. They roasted it over a ten-gallon drum out on the dock while Yuri re-enacted the shooting. One of the machinists got a hold of some pliers, yanked out a bloody tusk, and gave it to Yuri. An hour later and he had the thing on a necklace, yellowed and nested in his chest hair. When he saw me at the edge of the crowd alone and huddled over my food he brought me a piece of liver on a red plastic plate, along with some macaroni salad he'd made himself. We sat at the edge of the dock looking out across acres of dead grass cut into cells by chain-length fences. The cages held vast stockpiles of machinery all washed over with orange rust. There was nothing else to look at and all the fields and all the metal went on for miles.

"Gary," he said, meaning our boss, "is a terrible marksman. Even in the end, he must shoot the pig in the eye." Then he handed me a crumpled wad of tissue paper. Inside was the other tusk. Despite a few specks of dried blood, it had been polished into brilliance. It was the kind of primitive exchange you might see on TV between a cowboy and an Indian and it moved me deeply. He pointed at my plastic Green Lantern ring. "For make jewelry for wife." Then he doled out some more macaroni salad onto my plate.

* * *

Tuesday night Phil the skinhead was arrested for beating the shit out of his girlfriend's father, and for the rest of the week I got to drive Mean Green. Phil had staked his claim to the vehicle the day they first unloaded it, telling us no way was he going to let a bunch of spics and chinks pilot such a fine machine. He even spray-painted its name across the circuit panel. One time, when he caught me eating my lunch in the cockpit, he slung a cupful of Gatorade at my crotch and shoved me out onto the floor. But now he was gone and Mean Green was mine.

It was a remarkable vehicle. Unlike in a regular forklift, you stood up to drive Mean Green. It had an orange siren on top and a horn that beeped a beautiful electric chortle around every corner. Best of all, the cockpit went up with the forks. It was like piloting some fanciful Japanese robot. You almost wanted to check the controls for a button labeled LASER CANNON or TRANSFORM!

I was sky-high, loading up a pallet, when a Mexican kid named Elvis pulled his forklift up under me and got out. I didn't know his real name. Elvis was an amateur cartoonist and dealt a little around the warehouse but he was a nice guy nonetheless. His aunt had worked with us too and was sitting on her ass at home on a workman's-comp scam. Elvis and I had attempted that but failed miserably. He ended up with a foaming tetanus shot in the ass and I have to check in at this crappy little clinic once a week where a fat, hairy doctor with breath like tomato soup prods at my hamstring for five minutes before filling up a plastic baggie with prescription samples.

"I'm getting fired today. I just know it," yelled Elvis.

"I seriously doubt that," I said.

Elvis took out his sketchpad and I struck a heroic pose in the cockpit: crouched on one knee, an arm at my hip and the other resting on my thigh. I surveyed enemy terrain below, my face stern. Elvis had a real gift and I wanted to do everything in my power to help.

"Too much eyebrow!"

"How's this?"

"Oh, well that's very nice. Oh."

I could see the leathery wad of a bat hanging from the rafters in the corner. I started coughing and hacking, hoping that it would fly into the portrait and cast bizarre sepulchral shadows across my face. But it didn't move.

When Elvis was done, he rolled up the sketch in an empty plastic soda bottle and lobbed it up to me. It was my face and my pose but everything else was different. I was bald, with hair on my knuckles and someone's heart palmed in my hand. Elvis said that he could let me have it for five bucks.

"Your chin works very nicely," he called out.

"You think so?"

"Most definitely."

Right then I heard Dennis the safety guy shouting something. I couldn't hear what he was saying. I looked down and saw him slapping the sketchpad out of Elvis's hand. Then he looked up at me and did this irate pantomime of invisible suspenders stretching out from his chest. The harness! I'd stopped wearing it because of how it mashed up my balls. But now I was looking at my fourth OSHA safety violation in under six weeks. There wouldn't be a fifth: my ass was grass. Elvis's too. Everyone knew it. "Come down!" Dennis shouted. "Now!" I shook my head like a child refusing a casserole. I was close to tears. I sat down Indian style, my knees quaking, and gripped the edges of the pallet. My nails dug into the wood.

I couldn't look down anymore. Instead I looked out to the east dock and saw Yuri strolling back from the break room with a burrito in his hand. He waved the burrito at Dennis and approached him. Dennis said something and then pointed up at me. Yuri looked up, then put a hand on Dennis's shoulder. He gave him a pat. It was a friendly gesture, a peace offering. In reply Dennis pushed a finger into Yuri's chest. Nobody liked Dennis because he was both pedantic and a suspected homosexual. Yuri must have felt the same way because I saw something in him go tense. He bit off a chunk of his burrito and spat the wad within a few inches of Dennis's boots.

Then Yuri said something to Elvis, and Elvis got back into his forklift. Yuri handed his burrito over to him for safekeeping and calmly put a foot up on each fork. He looked at Elvis and shot a finger straight up in the air. Elvis looked at Dennis. Before Dennis could say anything, Yuri shouted "Up!" and up he went.

He ascended to just a few feet away from me. "Hello Daniel," he said. At that point he could have seen from my smeared complexion that I'd been crying.

"Hello, Yuri." His short legs were stretched between the forks, and he had one hand clutched to the backstop grille. Other than that, he was a man without a net, fifty feet up. One look at him dangling there was enough to make my lunch bubble up my throat.

"Daniel, may I see your order?"

"Sure," I said. I wadded up the order and tossed it to Yuri. He caught it like I'd thrown him the keys to a sports car. He flattened out the paperwork and proceeded to pick the rest of the order, his legs locked into a split, placing carton after carton onto the forks. He stacked them up as high as himself, balancing them perfectly on two six-inch-wide prongs while Dennis shrieked something unintelligible from below. Then he pointed at the boxes on my pallet and squatted into a catching posture. He clapped his hands together and the sound of that thunderbolt shot me straight up to my feet. "Throw. I will catch," he said. So I lobbed them at him. With every toss I thought I'd knocked him off balance and sent him to his death, but it didn't happen. Yuri stacked the entire order across those two slender forks. I felt extraordinarily brave.

We went down together. The whirring of our machines in descent synchronized into a heavy buzz that announced our safe return to everyone. Gary was waiting with Dennis. Dennis opened his mouth to say something but Gary shot him a look.

Elvis and some of the others looked at us like our spaceship had just landed. He presented Yuri with the half-eaten burrito. We walked right past them all, into the hazy light of the break room, where strange music trilled out into the warehouse and made my shoulders clench up.

So I invited Yuri to dinner. He told me that he'd drive over in his carpet-cleaning van, a recent investment he'd made with another Slavic immigrant. He promised a free cleaning for me and my girlfriend. He showed up twenty minutes early and pulled his royal-blue van into my neighbor's driveway.

At dinner he showed us a picture of his wife, who was moon-faced. I suppose most people would call her fat. She was in medical school in Macedonia and her name was Svetlana.

"Medical school is very difficult, very intense in Macedonia," Yuri said.

"Oh, I believe it!" Kay said.

"Is it much different than it is in America?" I asked.

"Oh, very much so. I'm sorry to say yours is a confused system! But we lack money, resources. We must dig graves for study. In Macedonia, the graveyards are not like here. Not neat and in rows. Just a big mess, piles of bones underneath."

"You dig up graves?"

"Yes. To assemble skeletons."

"You grave-rob?" I said. "Your wife's a grave-robber?"

"There is nothing to rob."

"Daniel," Kay said, turning to me. Then she looked at Yuri.

"Just the bones, right?"

"Oh, we take the bones. Doctors need bones to study anatomy."

"Well that's perfectly understandable. You can't have a bunch of quacks running around who've never studied bones," Kay said.

He picked up a purple-boned piece of chicken. "We gather complete skeletons if possible. Then we boil the bones to clean them, to sterilize. Then we put a kind of, a substance."

"A lacquer?"

"Yes! A lacquer! I paint all the bones like this." He made a painting motion over the chicken bone and hummed. "And then they dry and my wife can continue her studies."

"Hey. I would kill for a cup of coffee," I said.

"My wife," said Yuri. "She has been through much. I cannot even tell you."

But then he told us anyway.

Svetlana's little cousin. Trapped under rubble. Found by a squadron of Serbian soldiers. It was a story about war and loss and death that was so perfectly pitched in its calamitous inhumanity that I couldn't think of anything to do but get up and feed the dogs while Yuri sat there, his head in his hand, my girlfriend stroking his thumbs. I waited in the utility room doling out brown slop, Dog 2 circling my ankles. Yuri came in and apologized.

"Oh no, it's okay."

He sniffed. "It is impolite of me."

"No no, the dogs just get hungry. If we don't feed them, all hell breaks loose."

He bent down and pulled the dog's tail out, inspecting the hindquarters. "But I must confess," he said. "The boy I spoke of, he was considerably younger."

"Oh, that's okay."

"Considerably. And he was aware," he said.

"Oh."

"I did not want your girlfriend to think he was conscious. But he was. Very much so. It is something we must not speak of to women."

"I appreciate that," I said. "Hey, let's take a look at that van of yours."

We went out to Yuri's van. I kept my distance and sipped coffee from the driveway. Kay crawled in with him. He showed us the tubes, the hydraulic sanitation motor, the apparatuses and brushes and how they connected. He held up a sudsy brush. "Dogwash?" he said. I looked to Kay with hopeful eyes but she shook her head.

Kay tried to keep up with us but that night we hit the vodka like old pros and I had to help her to the bedroom while Yuri fiddled with the stereo. When I came back in Yuri had sunk into the recliner, Dog 1 straddled across his thigh, curling itself into Yuri's massive palms. With closed eyes, Yuri lifted his hand in the air. "Jimmy Page," he said. "There is no equal."

I watched as he floated his hand in the air, trailing musical patterns, punctuating notes with a closed and righteous fist. I scooted my chair toward his until our knees touched.

"Yuri, I have to tell you something," I said. "Something bad."

Yuri opened his eyes and the recliner sprang up and Dog 1 tumbled down his legs. "Yes? I will listen."

"I've been sleeping with this girl in my neighborhood. High-school girl," I said. "I think she's pregnant." None of this was remotely true. I had never even seen a teenager in my neighborhood.

Yuri slapped my face. Then in the same motion, he put his hand on my shoulder and gave it a squeeze. Tears welled up in his eyes. Then mine. "Oh Daniel," he said. "You have made a mistake. A terrible mistake."

We talked for hours, but mainly I listened. He told me what a thug he used to be and about the men whose faces he had unjustly demolished. He showed me tattoos that looked like the kinds of things I doodled on the backs of notebooks. He told me about meeting Svetlana after a bomb had torn a wall off her kitchen. How he made a stew for her family out of rationed potatoes and shrapneled dogs he'd scavenged. He told me about training for the Olympics. I cried until I choked, and Yuri swatted my back until I could breathe again.

Later that night I drew invisible pictures on my girlfriend's back, connecting moles to other little splotches of discoloration while she made *hmm* noises. I tried to keep my body still and in one position. But that just made the bed heat up faster. It was nearly three in the morning when I angled an erection against her ass, hoping to awaken her into a sultry dreamlike fuck that she couldn't refuse. But she just coughed and continued her noises and that was that.

That night I dreamt as always of the wagon trains and the long-faced enforcer who approaches as I lie trapped under my fallen horse. "My horse is sick and needs water," I say, before he takes out his pistol and blows my head off.

Yuri had his accident the next morning. For once I was in the Vietnamese break room, trying to exchange a cup of Gatorade for a bowl of noodles, when we heard the scream.

He was next to the sorter, his body slumped over the railing, his right arm plunged deep inside the machine. With his free hand he pulled and pinched frantically at his jeans. Black smoke was fuming up over his chest. He tried to shake the cloud from his face, coughing, but it wasn't doing any good. I ran to his side, careful to keep my face out of the smoke.

"Yuri," I said. He dangled his head in response. Sweat, tears, and snot were slung from his face, pitter-pattering into the sorter. I reached my arm down with his, where the green and blue swirls of his tattoos disappeared into the machinery. I could feel the point where it had bitten into his flesh, past flaps of skin and greasy tendons.

A squadron of workers surrounded us, trying to dismantle the sorter while Yuri and I sank deeper into the core of this disaster. I put my arm around him and pulled him into me: one arm across his belly and the other gripping his wrist. He'd vomited into the machine and onto his chest and the smell mixed with the smoke was like no other. It was the kind of pungency that could pluck you from time and space and set you wherever it pleased. I felt my mind rocketing out of my body and into a construction completely alien to my own. I was piloting something magnificent and I did not want it to end. I gave up avoiding it and let the smoke waft up my nose until I was entirely fused within the moment.

Yuri came back for a moment. "I will try to let go of the wrench," he said. "Okay?" He sounded like a record being played backward.

"Okay," I said. He shifted his weight to his right side. Then I felt his body jiggle. The machine pulled his arm in another inch and a tiny wisp of blood spouted onto my neck.

"I cannot," he said.

"You shouldn't move."

"I will be still."

I could hear Elvis's voice. Someone was shouting instructions at him, telling him how to disassemble one of the motors. Elvis sobbed and gasped in reply. But the squiggly directional arrows and crudely rendered circuit diagrams that Anders had left taped to the gearbox were indecipherable, the ball-point ink smudged and the paper crackled from months of water damage. Elvis was scared, but I hoped he was taking it all in. I wanted to see how he would render the scene in the gray swooshes and curves of his portraiture, how Yuri's chin looked resting in the crook of my elbow, how my arm ran down the length of his, the egg-shaped bloodstain on my shirt. I wanted him to get it all exactly right.

THE
TOWER

<small>STEVEN MILLHAUSER</small>

DURING THE COURSE of many generations the Tower grew higher and higher until one day it pierced the floor of heaven. Amidst the wild rejoicing, the overturned flagons and the clashing cymbals, a few thoughtful voices made themselves heard, for the event had long been anticipated and was known to be attended by certain difficulties.

No one could deny, for example, that the remarkable height of the Tower, which was undoubtedly its most striking and brilliant achievement, was itself a cause for concern, since those who lived on the plain below couldn't possibly climb to the top within the short space of a lifetime. Inhabitants of the city or the surrounding countryside could at best begin the upward journey, without the slightest hope of nearing the end. Otherwise they could do nothing but remain where they were and wait impatiently for news to reach them from above. Even those who had taken up residence in the Tower could in no way be assured of success—many were now too old for climbing, others lived too far from the top, while still others, though vigorous and within reach, had lost their early fervor and chose not to continue the arduous ascent. It was soon clear that only a small number of devout pilgrims were likely to arrive at the ultimate destination, in addition of course to the company of workers who had completed the final stages of the Tower and were in fact the first to enter the domain of heaven. But the workers were slaves, trained by masons to lay brick upon fire-baked brick on a coating of bitumen, and otherwise uneducated, superstitious, and unreliable. It came as no surprise that their reports were unsatisfactory, especially since their words were passed down from person to person, sometimes shouted at a distance or repeated by a half-drunk servant, and thus hardly more trustworthy than an outright lie. Those living on the plain heard of a brightness, a radiance, a luminous whiteness, but it wasn't clear what the first visitors actually saw, if indeed they saw anything, although one report, greeted with a mixture of eagerness and distrust, spoke of streets paved with emeralds and gold.

Because the Tower had been the one great fact in everyone's life during the immense period of its construction, the problem of ascent had been discussed almost from the beginning. When, after several generations, the Tower had reached a certain height, mathematical calculations proved that no one could climb even that far in the course of an entire lifetime. A number of families therefore came to a decision. They chose a son and his bride and instructed them to climb as far as possible into the inconceivably high yet still far from complete Tower, there to settle in one of the new chambers that had begun to be fashioned for townspeople with a taste for height. In their new quarters they were to bear children, who in turn would one day continue to ascend. In this way a family could climb the Tower in carefully regulated stages, generation after generation.

But this method of ascent led to a second problem, which hadn't been anticipated. As dwellers on the plain climbed the Tower, their relation to the world below became less and less definite; after a certain point, a climber understood that he could no longer return to the plain during his lifetime. Such people, and there were many, found themselves neither on earth nor in heaven, but in some in-between realm, in which it was easy to feel deprived of the pleasures of both places. One solution to this problem was for people to remain in a comparatively low portion of the always rising Tower, too high to descend to the plain, but close enough to those below for tales of the plain to reach them within a reasonable stretch of time; meanwhile, from a much greater distance, reports of heaven could find their way down. The drawback of this solution was that the farther from the top a climber found himself, the less reliable the reports from above were likely to be. For this reason, many in-betweeners climbed as high as they could, in order to be closer to the upper reports, with the corresponding disadvantage of receiving from below reports that grew less trustworthy as the height increased.

Just as the problem of reaching the top of the Tower had led to a number of unforeseen difficulties and confusions, so a host of purely technical problems had arisen during the long labor of construction. The original plan had called for a spiral ramp running around the outside of the Tower, along which lines of workers could transport fire-baked bricks and buckets of bitumen. But at the height of a thousand feet—a height three times greater than any tower had ever attained—it became clear that the original calculations had failed to anticipate the actual strains on so vast a structure. It was therefore necessary to widen the base to nearly four times its original dimensions—a labor that caused the destruction of large sections of the city. And so a second Tower, as it were, grew up around the first, to the height of a thousand feet. At that point a single Tower continued to rise, but now containing an inner ramp that was the continuation of the original outer pathway. The Tower now had two circular paths, an inner and an outer, both of which were used by workers who, as the Tower rose higher, began to work inward from the outer ramp, and outward from the inner ramp, and who began to leave, along the inner ramp, small hollows used as storage and resting spaces.

As the Tower rose still higher, workers encountered another problem. How could they transport new bricks to the always rising top of the Tower? For already, even at this very early stage of construction, it took many days for the bricks to be moved from the kilns in the brick-makers' workshops to the upper rim of the Tower, by means of solid-wheeled carts pulled by two men round and round the gently sloping ramps. The problem was solved by assigning special workers, called carriers, to levels separated by thousand-foot intervals. From each level the carriers moved bricks to the next carrier above, who brought them to the next carrier, and so on. The carriers, who of necessity became permanent dwellers in the Tower, enlarged the storage and resting spaces into primitive dwelling places, which later were elaborated into one of the Tower's most striking features.

For once the carriers had begun to live in the Tower, bringing with them their wives and children, the notion of permanent residence began to take hold. Toward the end of the second generation, when the Tower was already so high that it disappeared into the brilliant blue sky, like a long pole thrust into deep water until the end trembles, shimmers, and vanishes entirely, the King of Shinar, renowned for his piety, ordered workers to prepare a court high in the clouds, where he intended to spend his remaining days in fasting and prayer. When the court was ready, the forty-year-old king left his palace, and, in the company of his queen, his sons, his diviners, his concubines, his courtiers, his menservants, and his musicians, began the long climb up the inner ramp of the Tower; by the time he arrived in his new quarters he was an old man, his queen long dead, his sons solemn with middle age, but he took up residence in the broad halls and richly appointed chambers that stretched away on both sides of the inner ramp.

News of the high court spread quickly. It soon became fashionable for merchant families and even skilled laborers to arrange for living quarters within the Tower, far above the roofs of the temples and the royal palace, higher than the smoke of sacrificial fires, higher, it was said, than the dreams of young women fetching water from wells on rich blue summer afternoons. In this manner the city on the plain was gradually drawn inside the great

Tower. The Disappearance, as it was later called, came about in part because of the example of the pious king, but in part, too, because it was terribly oppressive for people to live at the foot of an enormous heaven-seeking Tower, which threw its shadow farther than a man could travel in a month and which, even at a distance, loomed like a raised arm about to strike a blow. Slowly the dwellings of the city were abandoned, the streets deserted, the gardens run to seed; the poor now gathered in ramshackle huts attached to the vast base of the Tower; after a time there was nothing left in the ruined city but wild sheep and lean oxen roaming the weed-grown streets, frogs in the wells, snakes and scorpions in the abandoned temples and dwelling places.

But no sooner had the Tower swallowed the city than a new desire arose, which no one could have foreseen. Even those who had thought long and hard about the Tower, in the days when the city flourished—the temple priests, the royal household, the administrative officials, the chief scribes—even they had failed to imagine one small but eventful change: a gradual loss of mystery and power in the glorious structure that rose higher than the flight of eagles but that had come to seem, as the years passed, just a little familiar. The Tower had, after all, been in existence for as long as anyone could remember. Although it was growing higher, day by day, it was always the same size to those within it and even to those few who had remained in the surrounding countryside, for the work at the top took place in invisible regions far beyond the range of earthbound sight. At the same time, even among people who believed firmly that the

Tower would one day reach heaven, the early expectation of a rapid and almost miraculous success had long been abandoned. It was therefore natural enough to feel that the rise toward heaven was, in a sense, part of the unchanging essence of the Tower, that the act of completion belonged to a different tower, a dream Tower, a Tower out of childhood stories, and was in any case an event so far in the future that it no longer had direct force in the lives of any but a handful of fanatical believers. There thus arose, in the hearts of the Tower dwellers, a nostalgia for the plain, for the shouts of the marketplace, the sunlight falling past the awnings onto heaps of apricots and figs, the sun and shade of the courtyards, the whitewashed temples, the outlying gardens shaded by date palms. And it came to pass that after a time many of the Tower dwellers began to descend and take up their old lives in the shadow of the Tower, rebuilding their ruined homes, planting their gardens outside the city walls, and gathering daily around the stalls in the market.

When, therefore, the Tower was completed, it contained a considerable population who lived on nearly every level, in chambers varying from primitive caves to rich halls painted with red, black, and lapis-blue hunting scenes, above a thriving city that had already forgotten its earlier abandonment and decay. The news of the successful completion led to a number of immediate changes. The city dwellers, who for their entire lives had scarcely given a thought to the perpetually unfinished Tower in their midst, suddenly stared up at a new, mysterious Tower, an unknown Tower, a Tower that had sprung out of the old one in a single, exhilarating leap. Tower fever swept the populace. Helplessly caught up in the new upward-flowing excitement, people began the impossible climb, without any hope of reaching the top. Meanwhile those already living in the Tower were shaken by the news—some rushed to begin the final ascent, others, far below, drove themselves to climb higher, while still others, though remaining in their chambers for reasons of health or spiritual feebleness, kept raising their eyes nervously, as if their ceilings would burst, as they awaited word from returning travelers.

And the travelers returned. It was all a little puzzling to those who didn't travel, and even to the travelers themselves. No one, to be sure, had spoken of remaining permanently in heaven, in the days of the rising Tower. But the vision of a new life in the upper world had always shone out as a promise, especially to families who had climbed higher in successive generations and were waiting for the news that heaven had at last been reached. Now the way was suddenly open, yet there proved to be little inclination for settlement. People rushed in, stayed for a few days, or a few years, and then returned, with the exception of a handful who disappeared and were said to have lost their way in those white, unmapped spaces. Of the many reasons for return, two made a deep impression on those who were waiting anxiously for news from above. First, when all was said and done, when experiences of every kind were taken into account and carefully considered, the upper realm was somehow not what anyone had been led to imagine. The many reports of a brightness, of a blinding radiance, while attractive in their way, tended to suggest an absence of objects, a lack of the visible and tangible, which however wondrous was also somewhat tiring. Even those who claimed to see angels and gates of sapphire and streets of gold, or those who, seeing nothing but brightness, were filled with unspeakable bliss, soon came to feel that heaven, in some indefinable but unmistakable way, was unsuitable for permanent residence by the living.

The second reason took many by surprise. Those who flung themselves headlong into heaven discovered that they still carried with them, however dimly, images of the life their forefathers had left behind, down there on the legendary plain. So in the hearts of even the most fervent pilgrims there existed a counterpressure, a tug downward, toward the half-remembered land, the place of origin.

Thus it came about, after the completion of the Tower, that there was movement in two directions, on the inner ramp that coiled about the heart of the structure: an upward movement of those who longed to reach the top, or to settle on a level that would permit their children or their children's children to reach the top, and a downward movement of those who, after reaching the top, longed to descend toward the plain below, or who, after climbing partway, felt a sudden yearning for the familiar world.

But these two movements, which together constituted a vertical way of life, were offset by a third movement. Many inhabitants of the Tower who had taken up permanent residence in order to prepare for the ascent of the next generation were too old, or too tired, or too distracted by the life around them, to desire a change in either direction. And so, in addition to the upward and downward migrations, which took place along the inner ramp, there was a horizontal life that flourished in the many chambers that stretched away on both sides of the inner ramp on every level, to the center of the Tower in one direction and to the outer edge in the other. The horizontalists raised children, visited back and forth, and engaged in a communal life much like that of the city far below. Metalworkers, goldsmiths, leather-workers, weavers, and reed-workers set up workshops and did a thriving business. Communities of tenants established small gardens and sheep pens, to supplement deliveries of grain and fruit from the distant plain. Sometimes, in the bustle of daily life, a Tower dweller would recall the fabled structure stretching high above, impossibly high, all the way to heaven, and would grow quiet for a time.

Although the two ways of life, the vertical and horizontal, proceeded independently within the Tower, they intersected at the arched doorways of chambers directly bordering the inner ramp, where travelers passed up and down. After a while the borderers began to offer inexpensive meals to hungry travelers, who were tempted by the great tureens of soup and the loaves of unleavened bread baking in clay ovens to rest awhile on their upward or downward journeys. For an additional fee, posted on wooden signs, travelers could sleep beneath goat's-hair blankets in chambers furnished with reed mats, wool rugs, or mattresses filled with straw. Sometimes a traveler, weary of the long journey, and yielding to the seductive peace of the chambers, chose to stay and become a member of the horizontal world; now and then a chamber dweller, stirred by the continual movement of travelers making their way to the top or descending toward the plain, joined the upward or downward flow. But in general the two ways of life opposed each other in equal measure, within the great Tower, as if the two lines of force were part of the system of architectural stresses crucial to the cohesion of the building.

Because of the extreme height of the Tower, which always disappeared from view and therefore was, for the most part, invisible, it was inevitable that rumors should arise concerning its permanence and strength. Cracks appeared in chamber walls, chunks of brightly colored glazed brick on the exterior wall broke off and fell onto the outer ramp, where they occasionally tumbled along and startled travelers, and in the high winds of the upper regions the Tower often swayed, causing ripples of panic among the inhabitants, while those who lived on the plain below, looking up, seemed to see, just beyond the limits of their sight, an entire world about to fall. Then teams of workers would swarm up along the outer ramp to repair the cracks, replace the damaged bricks, and strengthen broad sections of the Tower by propping the inner walls with powerful cedar beams that came from the mountains of Lebanon. On the plain below, an early system of soaring buttresses—a stupendous architectural feat in itself—was reinforced by a massive array of additional supports, which extended high over the streets, over the temples and the royal palace, the river and the marketplace, reaching beyond the fortified walls of the city, out into the distant countryside.

Meanwhile reports of heaven continued to sift down through the Tower, and reports of the plain drifted up, at times mingling and growing confused. People began to dream of climbing to the top of the Tower and entering a world of green fields and flocks of sheep, or descending to a land of blinding radiance. In this swirl of downward nostalgia and upward longing, a curious sect arose, deriding the delusions of climbers and proclaiming that heaven lay below—a wondrous place of twisting streets, marketplace stalls heaped with fruit, and two-story houses with wooden galleries running along inner courtyards. But this was only an extreme instance of the many common confusions of that time. Reports of heaven by actual visitors often seemed unconvincing or deceptive, while people who had never left the Tower began to add colorful touches and even to invent journeys of their own. For the tale-tellers, many of whom came to believe their own stories, heaven was always a sensual delight, a city whose great gates were covered with emeralds and sapphires, beryl and chrysoprase, topaz and jasper, while inside rose towers of silver and gold. The imaginary heaven proved far more compelling than the reported one, which was difficult to visualize and in any case had become half dream by the time it reached the lower regions of the Tower; and if the mixture of elaborations, inventions, distortions, and truths stirred in some a desire to see for themselves, in others it produced a tiredness, a spiritual heaviness, which led them to forgo the exertions of the vertical life and to rest content with the milder, more tangible pleasures of a horizontal existence.

It was about this time that the first rumors arose concerning deeper flaws in the Tower. The cracks, the pieces of fallen brick, even the swaying itself, were said to be common and superficial signs, true of every building, whereas the great Tower, which rose so fearfully high that it attained a different order of being, was subject to stresses and strains unknown to the architecture of the everyday world. There was talk of a hidden flaw, a continuous line or fracture running along the entire length of the Tower, somewhere on the inside; and although no one was able to point to the line itself, it was said that, if you listened closely, you could hear, deep inside the Tower, a faint sound like the creaking of many ships in the harbor beyond the marketplace.

What had the dwellers on the plain expected of heaven? Some had hoped to penetrate a mystery, others to outwit death—as if, by appearing bodily in heaven, they would no longer be required to die—still others to take part in a grand adventure, some to be reunited with those who had been buried in the earth, others to feel happiness after a life of hardship and sorrow. If heaven did not directly disappoint every expectation, it was also somehow not what most people had looked forward to, during the generations of hope. What could they make of that white radiance? One difficulty, debated at length by the temple priests, was that the heaven witnessed by travelers was not necessarily the true heaven, which some insisted was inapprehensible by the senses and could be known solely by the spirit unencumbered by the body. According to this argument, even those pilgrims who saw shining towers and heard choruses of unearthly music were deceived by organs of sense that could not but distort the experience of a nonterrestrial and immaterial place.

In the midst of such discussions, it was perhaps not surprising that the Tower itself should be called into question. Troubling whispers began to be heard. Was it possible that the great Tower didn't actually exist? After all, no one had ever seen the entire structure, which kept vanishing from sight no matter where you stood. Except for a handful of visible bricks, the whole thing was little more than a collection of rumors, longings, dreams, and travelers' tales. It was less than a memory. The Tower was a prodigious absence, a soaring void, a pit dug upward into the air. It was as if each part of the visible Tower had begun to dissolve under the vast pressure of the invisible parts, operating in every direction.

A time soon came when all those who had been alive during the completion of the Tower passed into the enigma of death, leaving behind a new generation, who had never known a world without the perfected Tower. The other Tower—the striving Tower, the always rising and changing and ungraspable Tower—retreated into the realm of hearsay, of legend. Now the new Tower was the stuff of daily life: an immobile Tower, rigid with completion. Though not without splendor, it lacked the sharp mystery of unachieved things. Even the ascent to heaven no longer seemed remarkable, though travelers still returned with tales of a dazzling radiance. As for the descent to earth, it had become little more than a humdrum journey, a change of residence such as many inhabitants of the Tower undertook from time to time.

And a listlessness came over the Tower dwellers, a languor of spirit, punctuated by bursts of excitement that quickly died away. People began to say that things had been better in the old days, before the Tower had brought heaven within reach. For in those days, they said, the dwellers in the plain lived in a continuous state of joyful anticipation, of radiant hope, as they stared up at the Tower that grew higher and higher in the bright blue welcoming sky.

But now a shadow seemed to have fallen across that sky—or perhaps it was a shadow across the heart, darkening the sight. People began to turn elsewhere for the pleasures of the unknown and the unseen. It was a time of omens, of dire prophesies, of feverish schemes that led to nothing. Passions swept through souls and ravaged them like diseases. A mother strangled her child when a man with wings whispered in her ear. A young man, declaring he had learned the secret of flight, leaped to his death from the outer ramp. One day a group of plains dwellers suddenly decided to escape from the Tower, which they said crushed them by its heavy presence. With tents and walking staffs they traveled across the countryside and out into the desert. Months from home, wandering exhausted in a strange land where cattle had horns twisted in spirals, where stones had the gift of speech, they looked up and saw the far Tower, rising forever into the sky like a howl of laughter.

Others, rejecting flight as useless, argued that a new work

was necessary, an all-consuming task as great as the Tower itself. In this way arose the idea of a second Tower—a reverse Tower, pointing downward, toward the infernal regions. People were struck with astonishment. How could they have failed to think of it before? The land of no return, the abode of death: the mere idea of it filled them with strange, delicious shudders. Everyone suddenly longed to wander in the domain of darkness, beneath the earth, where dim figures brushed past with haunted eyes. A wealthy woman in a high chamber held an Underworld party, in which guests came dressed as dark phantoms and pale corpses. Dim oil lamps cast a gloomy half-light. One young woman, of high beauty and mournful eyes, wore only her own flesh, as a symbol of all that passes away. Meanwhile an architect and three assistants drew up the plans of a new Tower; a committee gave its approval; teams of laborers began digging inside the base of the old Tower. They had gone down nearly two hundred feet before interest began to waver, excitement turned elsewhere, and the project was abandoned forever.

In this atmosphere of weariness and restlessness, of sudden yearnings that collapsed into torpor, the Tower itself was often neglected. Here and there old cracks reappeared in the bricks of a chamber wall, the inner ramp was riddled with hollows, glazed bricks on the exterior wall lost their luster and were severely damaged by wind and rain. Piles of rubble rose on the outer ramp. The workers, whose task it was to maintain the Tower, seemed to move slowly and heavily, as if the atmosphere around them had thickened; sometimes they sat down and leaned their heads back against the wall, closing their eyes. A rumor arose: the workers had all died, only their sad ghosts drifted along the spiral paths. In the innermost chambers, the Tower dwellers often felt drowsy and would nod abruptly into sleep, like children falling into a well. Later they would wake suddenly, looking about with startled eyes. Down below, in the city, a young girl dreamed that she was pouring water from a jar. As she poured, the water turned to blood. Inside the Tower, the sound of creaking ships grew louder.

One afternoon a boy playing in a street beside a whitewashed wall looked up at the Tower and did not move. Suddenly he began to run. In another part of the city, a woman drawing water from a well raised her eyes. The handle spun round and round as the bucket plunged. High up in the Tower a pilgrim on the inner ramp reached out a hand to steady himself against a wall. On a table in a high chamber, a bowl of figs began to slide. Down below, on one of the buttresses, a row of sparrows rose into the air with beating wings, like the sound of a shaken rug. A wine cup rolled along the floor, smacked into a wall. A wagon, beside a sack of grain, fell through the air. Far away, a shepherd looked up from his flock. He bent his head back, shading his eyes.

Frederiksborg

LOVE,
THE
FRONTIER

Emily Anderson

14 Feb

Love, I am coming out to you in my wagon. I hear the call of dense forests, gold, jackrabbit plains. Rare wildflowers, now extinct. Glances that irrigate deserts. Cities of prairie dogs cute as Valentines. Skies like an open pocketbook, held upside down and shaken. 25° F.

16 Feb

Also: threats of buffalo runs, Indians, cyclones. Cholera. Wildfires. I know the risks: suffering, death. Suffering worse than death. 35°, sunny.

18 Feb

I studied maps and charts, overland routes and a few across the waters at the bottom of the world. I read accounts: a woman who slept with the windows open in January and feasted on brains and butterfat to make the swim through the bergs, the water's surface like broken safety glass. Pa Ingalls survived three days of blizzard in a snowbank, eating the girls' Christmas candy. My windows are open. There are Hershey's kisses in my coat pockets. 28°.

29 Feb

Leap Day. Something is *different* about time. I am getting fed up with lonesomeness caught like hair at the back of my tongue. I stuck a for-sale sign in the rear window of my Ford Escort. 36°. Cloudy.

5 March

I closed my account at Fleet Bank and stuffed five hundreds into the toes of my boots. On eBay I sold almost everything: my television, bed, books, and CDs. 44° and sunny!

6 March

38°. Rain. Slept on the carpet. Woke up with blue fuzz in my nose. Traded a lock of my grandmother's hair, wrapped around an amethyst, for a Civil War musket, a bullet mold, and 2 cups of lead shavings.

8 March

39°. Rain. Ordered a prairie schooner from the Studebaker Brothers. *Conestoga.* Yankee bed. Jockey box. Iron brake. *Tongue.* Looking forward to frontier sex.

15 March

Dragged all trash I couldn't sell—a broken box fan, blades

black with dust, a leaning wire bathroom shelf, my parents' fifty-pound microwave—to my parking space and built a corral. Mudly and Studly, my new oxen, are huge and reportedly "docile," but they terrify me. Never even touched a cow, only chinchillas and Chihuahuas and cats. 50°. Fog.

16 March

60°!!!, sunny. Today I made a trough out of the gutter. I clogged the storm sewer with dirt and rotten leaves and let the spigot run. Mudly and Studly were glad to drink. My neighbors howled on the horns of their Jettas, trying to parallel park around my team. I petted my oxen. I am starting to like them.

22 March

40°. Partly cloudy. Early start 6 a.m. Uphill out of Boston. Team's breath fogged in the morning; rainbows came thru. Pines up here break with snow weight. Made camp 5 mi. out of Worcester. Chickens SCREAMED at every bump in the road. 0 eggs among the straw.

23 March

40°. Clouds, wind. 10 mi. TIRED.

24 March

50°. Sunny. Trees like Alcott. Pond like Thoreau. Found a bent nail in Studly's feed bag!?! Rescued him.

1 April
Todd,

    By now you've figured out I not only haven't been returning your calls, I am no longer a Sprint customer. This is because I have gone FAR AWAY. I'm looking for a Love you wouldn't be able to understand, let alone give. Facing dangers and hardships of all kinds for its glorious prospect. Something in the new grass gives my oxen bloat and foul humors. Barely made 15 mi. over 3 days. Wiped black strings from their mouths w/handkerchief. Learned to dangle a bullet from a stretch of twine and hypnotize them. When they blink and yawn, I place a pat of ginger on their big flat tongues. BIG sneezes! But ginger is v. good for the GI sys and I am getting to love them and if ginger doesn't work it means a big knitting needle, sharpened to a fine point, then sterilized by fire… Will mail this at Cleveland if I make it there.

    Love from the Frontier,
    Tori

5 April
60°. Rain. Coffee, molasses, flint, and stone, I am out here all alone.

1 May
MAY DAY!!! 85°!!! Sunny!!! Sudden heat caused the wheels to shrink up—the iron tires rolled right off them—I chased those suckers downhill with arms spread out and skirts flapping.

9 May

Dear Mom and Dad,

Reached Independence safely. 85°, fair and sunny. Ate a dish of new peas. Green tastes so good! I miss the produce aisles of home, but more than produce I miss you. Wish you were here to give me advice—now I am choosing among wagon trains. The one I will probably join is all women: Ashley, Pam, and Jamie & Lisa (sisters). We had a slumber party last night in my room at the Inn, and I made Mom's Girls'-Night Mai Tais, but something bothers me about Ashley. (She kind of reminds me of your old boss Debra, but maybe it is just her weight and I don't want to think I'm judgmental like that.) Oh well. Got to grow up sometime. Love you both,

Tori

20 May

86°. T-storms. Lost some weight today—sold my heavy loom, 200 lbs., to a couple that met up on the way out here. They're arm in arm like a yoked team: decided to get married, stay here, move in above the dry goods. He's a computer programmer and she's a social worker. My *oxen* are braver than they are.

3 June

80°. Humid. Lisa has cholera. Pam and Ashley: big fight. Pam: let's wait a few days for Lisa to get better. Ashley: throw her in the back of the wagon and *git*. (Dying regardless.) Jamie, Lisa's sister, doesn't say anything. Me neither. (Ashley's 6'1" and 220 lbs.) Went on, made 17 mi.

5 June

83°. Sunny. To keep wolves away from her body (only 90 lbs. when she died) we buried Lisa between the furrows of the road. The next company to pass'll grind her smell out of the dirt. Pam wanted to bury her by a creek with a cross but Ashley said no and Pam didn't say anything, just snorted and blew her bangs up and staked her picket-pin in the ground, *hard.* Then Jamie got hysterics. We boiled her some roots. Had to be held down to take infusion. Mudly has a limp.

8 June

90°. Sweaty. Gnats. Dreamed last night of Love. Made Mudly a splint of ash bark. 16 miles!

18 June

Ran into Pony Express man! Boy, really—Paul Revere, no rela-tion. He stopped a minute with us to wipe the lather from his mustang. Lonely. Told us jokes nonstop while his horse drank, then tipped his cap and left us with a pile of old Eastern newspa-pers to "curl our pretty hair with."

June 19
Dear Mom & Dad,

I found out about Nana in an old Boston Herald I came across on the prairie. It is only a coincidence that I even <u>know</u>*. I don't know what to say. By the time this reaches you, maybe your grief will be over. I read that the funeral was a month ago but right now I wish*

I was there, eating ham sandwiches and sweet pickles and hearing stories about Nana's vaudeville days, the time she fended off a baptism with a hat pin. I hope you are all taking good care of each other.

Love,

Tori

29 June

101°. Dry. No water but a stinking alkaline lake. Licked dew off the grass. A LITTLE water left in rain barrels, but no firewood to boil germs out.

30 June

101°. Same. Chickens dead of thirst. We lie in wagonshade. Mudly's and Studly's tongues ulcer with thirst. We drank our dirty water, all except Jamie, who prayed for Lisa to come and help.

1 July

102°. Dysentery. Got Jamie on best horse w/some hollow gourds. Go for help.

July 20

My two poor oxen who have never harmed anyone and do not deserve their awful fate. Dying alone on a treeless plain, I believed that Cupid had played a cruel joke. What scared me most was not dying, but *thirst.* If true love and a canteen had dropped from the sky, I wouldn't've shared even a drop with my beloved. For the first time I doubted my fitness for the Frontier.

Now that I am recovered, I know that diarrhea in a poisoned lake is not love. I know, too, my limits and am eager to overcome them. True love is only increased by obstacles.

At dawn on what could have been my last loveless day on earth, Jamie rode back with fifteen soldiers on fresh horses from Ft. Laramie. I thought the thunder of hooves was my heart's last hurrah, that the seventeen-year-old cadet who cradled my neck and pressed his cold canteen's mouth against my lips was an angel. He flung me up over his horse.

"But my team," I said.

"Hush now," said the cadet.

"My oxen," I said.

"Don't worry," he said.

I had no more strength to speak. My hair came undone and shook in the wind as we galloped over the plains. Only hours from death, our rescuers placed all five of us in the care of their "wives," who occupied a long log hut outside the stockade.

This hut was called the Hog Ranch. And they called their wives clementines.

The Hog Ranch had no windows, but stripes of light came through the chinks between the logs. The clementines were kind at first. Maude, who wore the Colonel's epaulettes like flowers in her hair, helped me lie down on her own straw tick, bathed me with cool damp rags, and applied hot poultices to my abdomen. At night the clementines sang us love ballads to help us sleep, then quietly opened the door for the men.

The soldiers brought the clementines plugs of tobacco, cold

flapjacks wrapped in handkerchiefs, handfuls of coffee beans. Through fever dreams I heard the men's noise and stirred. The clementines whispered, "Keep it down, boys; let's not wake the ladies."

With such good care, in ten days I went from a feeble 98 lbs. back to 110 on the commissary scale. The soldiers began to visit the Hog Ranch in the afternoons. They brought trinkets for us convalescents, bright buttons torn from their jackets, white sugar in paper packets.

My young cadet, Horace, gave me bunches of rough-stemmed wildflowers, their petals wilted and brown-edged by the sun. One evening he took my arm and walked me around the perimeter of the stockade, pointing out constellations in the big Wyoming sky. I was not yet strong and weary from walking, so I let him grope me up against the outhouse. He took me to dine with him in the mess. The scraps from the meal went first to the hounds, then to the clementines.

That night Maude dragged me out of bed and shoved me onto the dirt floor with a heap of greasy blankets that made me nervous about smallpox. We began to see the clementines for what they were: rough, sepia-skinned women, too worn by the stasis of their lives to smile. Their fishnets were torn and dirty, their mascara clumpy and full of germs.

I asked Horace one bright, hot morning if he would take me to the livery to see Mudly and Studly. "I would, but they are out to pasture, eating green grass and frolicking," he said.

It wasn't like Mudly and Studly to frolic. And I hadn't seen a blade of grass that wasn't brown. I insisted he take me to them.

"But you're too pretty to cry," said Horace.

"Where are they?" I said.

"Died of bloat yesterday," he said. "Sometimes the animals overfeed, after almost starving. I know a *lot* about livestock." He pulled me to him and pressed my face against his bony shoulder and began to rub my back, moving his hands over the ridges of my corset. "Hush now," he said, "hush." I pushed him so hard he staggered backward. Then I raced to the pump to wash the tears off my face.

Ashley was already there, sitting in the dust, weeping into her hands. Her huge shoulders shook under her calico. Her team, too, was dead. I put my arms around her and cried into her bun. Maude pushed past us toward the pump, knocking my collarbone with her empty bucket. "What are *you* crying about?" she said, violently jerking the pump handle.

"Our oxen died of bloat today," I said.

"How are we supposed to leave?" wailed Ashley. "I want to go *west.*"

Maude laughed and heaved up her bucket. "DUH, ladies," she said. "They never brought your livestock back. They wanted to keep you here. More snatch for them, less food for us." She spat, right in Ashley's face.

Ashley grabbed Maude by the collar of her halter top and lifted her, pail and all, into the air. Her little feet in button boots kicked into a blur. "Then *help us get out of here,*" Ashley said. She flung Maude to the dust.

That night, after the soldiers buttoned their flies and

returned to the barracks, we gathered—clementines and pio-
neers—in the center of the hut and conspired. Pam, the prettiest
and our lookout, stood outside the door and smoked a cigar.

Providence wasted no time. The very next day, a wagon train
passed through. Word went around that one of their company had
a crate of whiskey to sell for a dollar a pint. I took a hundred out
of the toe of my boot. We carried the liquor back in our aprons.

The festivities started before dinner, so the men wouldn't
have the advantage of full stomachs. Jamie, who had studied vio-
lin at Juilliard, played a jig on her fiddle as we got our soldiers
dangerous with drink. When Maude thrummed a march on her
snare the men took off in a line with their pistols. There were
some accidents. In the confusion, we hurried to the livery and
took what we could find: sixteen mules and four mustangs.

We located our abandoned wagon train by the stench. Poor
Studly and Mudly. Their carcasses, stripped by wolves and vul-
tures, were bare save for flies and maggots. I took a deep drink
from my canteen. It tasted like Horace. There was nothing to do
but go on. We hitched up our fresh teams and headed west.

29 July
80°. Rain, wind. Stepped in gopher hole. Ankle swollen, purple.
Barely walk. Have to ride and suffer the jolts.

1 Aug
Dear Sis,
    70°—chilly in the mountains! You should see my buff arms—it

takes a lot of strength to restrain the team on the downslopes. The reins tore the flesh off my palms, and Ashley rubbed my blisters with bear grease. Pam surprised me with a pair of leather gauntlets. Even though we're all looking for love, there's no petty jealousy. We'll all find our soulmates. There will be one for each of us, nontransferable. The air is so clear up here! You ought to come out.

Love,

Tori

5 Aug

70° and sunny. We stopped and camped by a clear creek with a huge company of Mormons. A moving city: hundreds of wagons, stench and noise. Stern men, dour women, flocks of children tearing off in all directions. We heard them for miles before we saw them. But after dinner, during their services, the whole company was quiet and we were too, out of respect. None of the women spoke to us Jezebels, but the kids stared. Some of the men approached us with a broken wagon wheel. Jamie had a spare, so she traded for a fabulous new musket.

One of the men was beautiful as the sea.

I can smell the salt. We must be getting close.

7 Aug

80°, light drizzle. Heard hoofbeats behind us today. Two riders galloped over the ridge, reined in and rode beside us. When they tipped their caps, I recognized one of them from the Mormon camp. Job. The whole day felt fast and anxious: the wind picked up at our backs and pushed us forward. We didn't speak, though Job whistled to his dogs, who retrieved jackrabbits from the tall-grass. He skinned and roasted them over the fire that evening. The smell of that fresh, sizzling meat! It had been a long time. As we ate, the men asked if they might join our company. Or one of them did—Job kept his peace, pulled the brim of his hat low over his face and whittled while Tyler made a speech about how he and Job had been moved to find God, but later realized it wasn't God they sought. Pam giggled. Job looked up at me and scraped a big chunk of wood off his carving. It flew into the fire and burned.

10 Aug

Job walked beside me all day. He smells so good despite hardship. 83°, 25 miles!!!

15 Aug

Job showed me what he has been carving: two small wooden hearts that fit inside a wooden box. When you shake the box, the hearts go beat-beat. 86°.

17 Aug

85°. Woke up to thunder. It was my turn to perk coffee and fry fatback, but I dropped the meat in the grass when I saw the dogs. Their throats were cut. Bright feathers floated in their blood.

Pam said she heard drums. Ashley said it was thunder. Tyler said if it were Indians, we'd best go back to the fort. Jamie said to get a move on. Job said we weren't going anywhere till we gave those dogs a proper burial.

He tried to hide his tears with his hat while he dug the graves for Haw and Gee. "You're perspiring," I said, and touched my last clean handkerchief to his cheek.

This is how we kissed. We forgot to cover up the graves. We even forgot the shovel.

18 Aug

89°. Dreamed I was being buried alive. Woke up with a mouthful of monogrammed white cotton. "You dropped your handkerchief," said Horace. I kicked, and he pinned me down. "Hanging's too good for horse thieves."

His mouth tasted like his canteen. "I'm taking you back to the fort." He dragged me from my wagon. In my place he left a handful of feathers and arrowheads.

19 Aug

91°. My boyfriend is an expert tracker.

Job spotted us on the bank of a stream. He shot his rifle in the air. "You killed my dogs." Horace fumbled with his revolver while Job splashed across the stream with his Winchester and his bowie knife.

20 Aug

Dear Mrs. Hardwick,

It is my sad duty to return to you your cadet's copper buttons, the paper money we found on him at the time, your own letters, kept close to his heart, and the blue ribbons from your county's fair: Horace told me he raised prize heifers. I knew Horace well. He saved my life. I once mistook him for an angel, which is, I'm sure, what he is now. I can say little that might console a mother about the cause of his demise, and feel certain there is no need to return to you the feathers and arrowheads found near him that must have belonged to his killers. Rest assured that an honorable, brave, and sensitive man—a dear member of our party—dug a grave, and you need worry about the dangers of the frontier no longer.

1 Sept

75°. Sunny. Lush green hills. Can smell the ocean! Scent of home and newness at once! I will stay here with Job and wait for the invention of the telegraph.

15 Sept
Dear Mom and Dad,

Safe in Seattle! Back to 130 lbs. Not that it makes any difference to Love! Plus Job has a saying about a plump wife and full barn… I know he doesn't mean the plump part, he only means the wife part, but no date yet… We are building a log home. Job whittled over 200 pegs himself to spare expense of nails! (We are broke.) But so happy. Got letter from Ashley. Seems she's had privations in Spokane but sounds hopeful/aggressive. Pam's camped nearby; says she's happy trapping and trading with Tyler, but Job says Tyler's not half the man he ought to be. Jamie went to Japan to learn how to become a sushi chef. I'm West, with Love!

Love from the Frontier,
Tori.

24 Nov

Sleet and 34°. But *someone's* getting his ass dragged out of a saloon anyway!

4 Dec

Rain. 34°. Found charred remains of 2 wooden hearts in the stove-ash.

20 Dec

Still raining. 32°. So much waterweight on the pine boughs the tree snapped and crashed through our roof. Woke up wet. Spent day stretching wagon bonnet over the hole. Couldn't get warm after.

23 Dec

30° F. Sleet. Grippe.

25 Dec

I told him I do not mind cold water up to the waist! I'd gladly pan for gold, spear salmon, or fell trees! I *told him.*

He won't get far. I smashed our one glass windowpane, sprinkled the shards into his boots.

Dec. 26

33°. Big, fat snow.

30 Dec

31°. Through thunder and stormwail, a knock on the door. Surprise,

surprise. He leaned on a crutch and held out peppermint sticks, wrapped in brown paper.

31 Dec

32°. Snowing. New Year's Eve! Popcorn and apple cider in our snug home. I heated water on the cookstove to dissolve the Epsom salts for Job's feet. Infection limned his toes with black. The fever gave him a firelit, summer complexion. We spoke of the Yukon.

3 Jan

It's a long, cold trip, and January's a bad season, but what are frozen fingers and failing matches compared to the Northern Lights of Love? Traded the wagon for a sledge, the mules for huskies.

10 Jan

Bought a hog. Butchered and trimmed it with Job's sharp knife.

13 Feb

Ready. Job's poor feet wither and dangle over the edge of the sledge. I stand in front in my sealskin cape, clutching my compass and crying *Mush! Mush!*

Freiberger

what

MAGDA
MARIA

Joyce Carol Oates

To Leonard Cohen

MAGDA MARIA, she was known to us in the early 1970s on River Street, in south Sparta. No one could have said what her last name was or where she'd come from, but her beauty was legendary even to those who'd seen her only at a distance, obscured by swirling clouds of smoke in the twilit River House barroom where she first appeared, in the company of an older man known to us as Danto (though Danto had no corresponding awareness of us). Danto was a massive man standing six feet two or three inches and weighing well over two hundred pounds in hand-tooled leather boots. Danto wore his hair long, though it was receding at the temples and defiantly threaded with silver, hair like the plumage of a splendid male bird, and Danto wore stylish clothes. He had a black leather coat with a sealskin collar and a low-slung ruby-red sports car whose exotic name few of us would have dared to utter aloud.

In one or another River Street tavern we drank away the hours like waders caught up in a pounding surf, or we traded drugs depending upon our desperation and recklessness and the shifting tyranny of our needs (drugs appeared in south Sparta the way, for some citizens, newspapers appear on the front stoops of houses). In the River House where time oozed, bent, collapsed into seconds, or looped back upon itself like rerun dreams, we had time to contemplate the beautiful doomed Magda Maria at the farthest end of the bar with her middle-aged companion Danto, eclipsed by his intimidating bulk, in silhouette unnervingly young, with the look both defiant and demure of a wayward schoolgirl. How was it possible, we wondered, that Magda Maria was served drinks at the River House?

She was prized for her waist-long shimmering-black hair, her face often obscured by curtains of it which from time to time Danto brushed with his fingers in a gesture of excruciating tenderness, that he might lean close to Magda Maria to whisper into her ear or kiss the edge of her mouth. Magda Maria was shy: was she? Magda Maria was unaware of our interest: was she? Or was Magda Maria well aware of us, casting us glances of intimacy and scorn, her face suddenly exposed, pale, doll-like? There were few other girls or women in the River Street taverns but some of them were painfully known to us, we'd bought them drinks, we'd gone home with them or had believed that we were meant to go home with them except something happened to intervene, we'd given them money or we'd stolen money from them, cheated them of drugs (nothing so precious as that few hours' happiness we took from them), but these girls and women were of little interest to us now that Magda Maria had entered our lives, for they were no longer beautiful enough or young enough or mysterious enough to be contemplated with yearning and lust. Instead there was Magda Maria arriving at the River House with her companion Danto, Magda Maria who came only just to Danto's shoulder, Magda Maria in an ankle-length black fur coat (mink?) that must have been given to her by Danto—somehow it was known that Danto owned clothing stores in Sparta, or Danto owned properties that leased space to clothing stores, he was a man with money, a man with the power of money, surely he was a man with a family somewhere, perhaps even close by, a man who'd sired children now grown and bitterly jealous of Magda Maria, a girl surely younger than his youngest daughter, and it was for such reasons that Danto adored Magda Maria as Magda Maria adored Danto. When Danto helped Magda Maria out of the black fur coat—tenderly he folded it beside them on a bar stool, where it seemed to drowse like a pampered beast—we saw that Magda Maria wore what looked like layered strips of cloth, flimsy as cobwebs, black muslin and black silk and black lace, a black skirt with a jagged hemline and an unexpected slit at the sides that exposed her beautiful pale legs, a black-translucent fabric through which Magda Maria's small ivory-white breasts shone and the shadows of her prominent collarbone could only just be glimpsed; and Magda Maria wore shoes with stacked heels, or boots with stiletto heels that caused her to teeter like a little girl in women's footwear.

It was believed that Magda Maria, with her straight shimmering-black hair and something resistant and prideful or arrogant in her manner, was of Indian descent, that she'd drifted down to Sparta from Rivière-du-Loup where there was a Seneca reservation, but no one could claim to know. Really no one could claim to have spoken with Magda Maria, for invariably in the River House Danto leaned possessively over her, shielded her from prurient eyes, held her attention by speaking to her in a ceaseless whisper to which Magda Maria only murmured in response, smiled, nodded, inclined her head in acquiescence, and if other men approached Danto spoke grudgingly with them and blocked their view and did not introduce them. We observed Magda Maria drinking—was it whiskey? straight whiskey?—as Danto drank whiskey—and imagined that should Magda Maria need to be rescued from her companion it would be to one of us she'd turn.

Those years love festered in me like a wound. I have to think that I died then, that what has survived is someone else.

Locust season! Panic hit me like a wave of filthy water, the things were everywhere and yet I could not assume that they were not inside my head and spilling out as other hallucinations had done in the past. I'd been sick then, and was possibly sick now, hearing shrieks in the trees, the things were falling onto my head and into my matted and unwashed hair. I was staggering along the riverbank kicking a path through locusts that lay an inch thick on the ground, some still alive and crawling over one another. *Seventeen-year locusts,* the most tragic of God's creatures, awakened in their cocoons underground with no way to eat, no mouths and only rudimentary eyes and sex organs encased in a shell, frantically digging their way to the surface to fly into the lowermost branches of trees careening like drunken pilots, crawling on trunks and tumbling over one another, blindly mating in a pandemonium of deafening shrieks after which the males began to shrivel and die almost immediately and the females lived a few hours longer in order to lay their eggs in the earth that the seventeen-year cycle might begin again immediately and then the females too began to die and by the next day the earth was strewn with the husks of locusts like discarded souls barred even from Hades this raw-aching morning after the news came to me that Magda Maria had died and while Magda Maria had not loved me in the past it was only now that it became impossible that Magda Maria would ever love me and in this way redeem me from the wreckage of my life bitter as bile in my mouth.

...in the River House Tavern, I saw her: Magda Maria! For rumors of her death were false, confused with a collapse, "rehab," and release. Something terrible had happened and Magda Maria was rumored to have died in what the newspapers called a *suicide pact,* her heart had ceased beating, yet somehow Magda Maria had been revived. It had been printed in the newspaper for all to see: Magda Maria's surname was *Huet,* her age was given to be twenty-five, *Maria Huet* had been taken into custody by Sparta police as a "material witness" and remanded by a judge to the Herkimer County Women's Detention, where voluntarily she entered a drug rehab program (alcohol, heroin) and after six weeks was released and living among us still, thinner than we remembered and more beautiful. It seemed unnatural: she had returned from the dead not at night but in the late afternoon of a mild day in March when most of the ice in the Black River had melted, and now she was standing not where Danto had invariably steered her but at the other end of the room, where waning sunlight from a stained-glass fanlight was reflected in the long horizontal mirror behind the bar and the rows of liquor bottles arranged before the mirror as on an altar sparkled and shone with the innocence of Christmas lights; and this light fell across Magda Maria's face which was subtly ravaged from death and yet radiant with the memory of death. Immediately the most aggressive of us, a man in his early thirties known on the street as D.G., stepped forward to buy Magda Maria a drink, a whiskey straight, and a whiskey straight for himself—already D.G. whose oily-blond hair was pulled back into a ponytail and whose jaws were covered in silvery-blond stubble had fallen in love with Magda Maria, would kill for her, though D.G. was notorious for his crude, cruel treatment of girls and women and had hurt certain of his associates and was the cause of others disappearing from Sparta and was a man to whom you did not wish to owe money unless you could repay it within twenty-four hours.

In her slow dazed seductive voice Magda Maria confided in D.G. that Danto had insisted that she die with him for it was time for them to die together, that Danto had poured whiskey into glasses for each of them to drink and emptied a bottle of barbiturate tablets for each of them to swallow down, for it could not be that they could live together, their love would become contaminated, the truest love is doomed. Life had become an irritant to him; his brain was steeped in whiskey, his eyes were jaundiced and his liver was enlarged and rode across the small of his back like a hard-rubbery leech. Magda Maria had pleaded with Herkimer County prosecutors to understand: she had not wanted to die, she had not wanted her fifty-one-year-old lover to die, she believed that suicide is a sin, except she could not bear to outlive Danto who'd adored her, she dared not outlive Danto who would return from death to curse her, it was a holy act between them, it was their only possible marriage, Danto was a Roman Catholic and all of his family was Roman Catholic and divorce was not possible for him.

In Danto's six-room "luxury" apartment on the top floor of a high-rise building overlooking the Black River in the old-city center of Sparta miles from Danto's suburban colonial home, on Danto's enormous bed covered in black satin threaded with gold, the doomed lovers lay together in each other's arms kissing and whispering and lapsing into sleep, after how much whiskey Magda Maria had been able to drink, how many barbiturates Magda Maria had been able to swallow before her throat shut against them and her bowels swirled with nausea. How close to death had Magda Maria come, lapsing into a twilight sleep wracked by coughing, choking, gagging, until at last Magda Maria began to vomit helplessly, vomiting up acidic whiskey and barbiturate tablets in chalky clumps as Danto sank ever more deeply into unconsciousness. Magda Maria thrashed in a delirium of physical distress, unaware of her (soiled, befouled) surroundings, fell back exhausted and wakened twenty hours later to a stench of vomit and excrement and there was a dead man heavy and stiffened in her arms and she could not move for a long time, she was partly crushed beneath the dead man's body, faintly she called for help uncertain if in fact she was alive or dead, trapped like this for what seemed a very long time, her throat raw, crying for help but there was no help, she could hear voices down on the street, she could hear traffic, she prayed, tried to pray, tried to work herself free of the dead man's embrace, his muscled arms gripping her, his heavy clammy-skinned face with eyes like mashed grapes oblivious of her, until at last she was on her hands and knees crawling across a patch of carpet calling for help and now someone outside in the corridor heard what sounded like a cat mewing piteously and finally she was discovered and an ambulance was called. But Danto was already dead, Danto had been dead for hours, Magda Maria pleaded that she had not wanted Danto to die, she believed that suicide is a sin and she had not wanted Danto to die and yet if Danto died it had seemed necessary for her to die, for she could not betray her lover even at the risk of condemning her soul to an eternity of hell, did he believe her?—Magda Maria's thin fingers now outstretched and pressed against D.G.'s chest in a gesture of childlike appeal and her dark-bruised eyes lifted to his face and suffusing him with the happiness of new, young love as more often he was suffused with the wish to do harm to another person, stammering to Magda Maria she was safe now, all that sick Danto shit was over.

And so she was back, though more frequently in the Black Bass where some of us were made welcome who weren't any longer at the River House where the bartender had taken an irrational dislike to us, and had threatened us. I wept to see Magda Maria still alive, returned to me though in the company of D.G. who sometimes spoke harshly to her, twisted her wrist or shoved her. Still Magda Maria was perceived to be young and beautiful if not so young and beautiful as she'd once been, her long loose black hair coarser now. Magda Maria's laughter was high-pitched and uncertain and Magda Maria's bruised-looking eyelids were often hooded as if sleep tugged at her, she would lay her head on her arms in dreamy exhaustion and D.G. might irritably prod and pinch her awake. By this time it seemed to be known among us that Magda Maria's family (a disappointment to us, who had not wished to believe that Magda Maria had any "family" to define her, as a net might be said to define a creature trapped and struggling inside it), French Catholics from Quebec who'd settled north of Plattsburgh, had disowned her years ago, when Magda Maria was a Catholic schoolgirl and had begun seeing an older man, no more than fifteen and already she'd begun drinking, she'd been using drugs, ran away with her lover to live in Massena, in Ogdensburg, in Old Forge, in Watertown, enrolling in one version of her story in the nursing school, for Magda Maria's wish was to become a nurse, or, in another version, posing as a (nude) model at the university's art school, ravishingly beautiful, very young, naïvely trusting and vulnerable, willing to pose naked before strangers, or in such need of money forcing herself to pose naked before strangers, and all of her (male) students fell in love with her, and one of her (male) instructors seduced her, a sculptor who also dealt drugs to undergraduates and was arrested and dismissed from the university. These years!—in which a doomed yet pitiless war was being *waged* in the cause of *democracy* on the far side of the earth by soldiers who were former classmates of ours, cousins, brothers who despised us, young Appalachian men, blacks who'd been drafted out of high school; we were shamed and exhilarated by our own moral rot, we were captivated by the prospect of early death yet at the same time in a permanent state of paranoia, believing that though some of us had minor criminal records or were recovering from hepatitis or were alcoholics whose brains had begun to shrink that we might yet be drafted into the army as it became increasingly desperate for soldiers, we would be forced to march in platoons in the zombie-uniforms of dead heroes who'd despised us. There must have been a time when we'd been students, and "promising": some of us had had scholarships, we'd been valedictorians of our high-school classes, but somehow we'd washed up in the shabby urban neighborhood south of the shabby campus of the state university at Sparta, an underfunded and generally reviled campus used formerly as a teachers' college. Some of us had been poets, artists, "intellectuals." Some of us had been graduate students, we'd been adjunct instructors at the university whose contracts had not been renewed. And yet a kind of hypnosis held us here in Sparta, a rain-washed city on the Black River, for here was the wreckage of our early promise. As in Hades visited by Odysseus and subsequently by Aeneas we were spirits of the dead and the damned clamoring for our lost lives in a perpetual trance of longing and there was Magda Maria we were in love with, Magda Maria who (we believed this) would forgive us our cowardice, Magda Maria who'd once been (we'd come to believe this) a nurse, like Dido who'd nursed the wounded Aeneas, saved his life and surrendered her very soul to him.

And the Black Bass was awash with expelled and exhausted souls, everywhere underfoot you kicked them inadvertently. These years!—yet they were happy years, though it was a matter of shame to the more sensitive among us that Herkimer County like most of rural America was filling up with war veterans not much older than we were, in some cases younger, shipped back from the far side of the earth maimed and broken and garlanded with glittering medals and eyes demented with chagrin, hurt, bafflement, rage. You would expect the vets to hate us as we hated ourselves, and some of them did hate us, but others unexpectedly became our friends and allies, drinking with us in the Black Bass, buying drugs from us or providing us with drugs, trading girls in the Cloverleaf down by the wharf, in Dunphy's on Quay Street which was partly burnt-out but open for business, and, as tides shifted, at the River House again where Magda Maria drank ever earlier in the day and less frequently with D.G. who'd been arrested, who'd been out on bail and arrested again and badly beaten by another drug dealer or by the Sparta police who were notorious for punishing "hippies"—"junkies"—"pimps"—in their energetic, practical way. And then D.G. vanished, was sent away to the men's maximum-security prison at Follette where he was killed by other inmates or by guards and Magda Maria, whose coat was now clearly not mink, not even fur, but something synthetic and glossy like formica, had been commandeered by a Vietnam vet named Ike with the baby-boy face of a battered Robert Redford, pitted skin and a patch of dirt-colored whiskers and endearingly shaky hands and a voice permanently hoarse from a war injury to his upper thorax.

Ike was a serious drinker, easy to befriend and not so proprietary of Magda Maria as her former lovers had been, in fact it was known (it was rumored, whispered) that Ike was living with Magda Maria in a house shared by others and Magda Maria was herself "shared" if circumstances veered in that direction. Magda Maria had herself been sick for a while, at the time of D.G.'s beating, and the shimmering-black hair had been cut in one or another medical facility but was now beginning to grow out again, not so profusely, brittle at the ends and giving off a rich, rankly oily odor that aroused me to such longing it was as if a demon had slipped inside me, down through my throat, into my body. It was believed by some that Magda Maria's mouth was no longer beautiful, ringed as it was with reddened sores, but I could not look away from that mouth, I was transfixed. Because Ike was present we could not speak to each other but had to communicate in more subtle ways and so I was spared the stammering banality of *I love you, I've loved you since the first time I saw you Magda Maria please will you love me?* For there was a part missing somewhere inside me, only in Magda Maria could this missing part be retrieved like a jigsaw puzzle piece kicked beneath a table. *Not this man, not this brute but I am your lover Magda Maria, I would die for you.* Within months Ike would become my enemy, Ike would take my money and sell me diluted goods like you'd sell under-graduates, coke laced with talcum powder or something worse, and later when Sparta police banged me around in the rear of the station house where they'd brought me "on suspicion" I would be determined at first not to give anybody up, I wasn't that kind of person, yet somehow seconds into the beating I would give up Ike Balboa's name, a name already well known to Sparta police, sobbing, so frightened of being hurt even more I'd have given up the name of my closest friend if I'd had a close friend. But that evening at the River House none of this would have seemed possible to me.

Magda Maria! Love me, we can save each other. Magda Maria understood my plea as clearly as if I'd spoken aloud. That evening

I leaned toward her, inhaling the oily-rank odor of her hair, her body, seeing how the filmy black-translucent shawl wound about her upper body had been sprinkled with glitter, tiny moons or mirrors, there were cheap clattering bracelets on Magda Maria's thin wrists and her small ears glittered with gold piercings and around her neck was a meager gold chain and on her breast-bone a small gold cross. Magda Maria was lifting her whiskey glass with a slow shaky hand and I saw that her fingernails had been polished red but were now chipped and broken, I wanted to kiss her fingers but instead I lifted my glass to click against hers, a gesture of sudden collusion, knowing that Ike was too drunk to observe, such love for Magda Maria pumped in my heart!—and Magda Maria smiled quickly and shyly as if I'd spoken her name, smiled at me with her beautiful wounded lips *Yes I can love you, I have been waiting for you, we will save each other.* Ike was joking about the steel plate in his head, saying how his skull had been cracked and some of his brains had leaked out, you could see a shallow, slightly discolored indentation in Ike's forehead like the place where a third eye might have been, now sunken in and the skin grown over mysteriously scarred and ridged.

...so close to the country you had only to drive over the Quay Street bridge and within a mile or two you were outside the city limits, following the Black River into a steeply hilly landscape of ancient glacier fields, small mountains, hills strangely shaped as if the earth had been bulldozed to no purpose other than to disfigure it. Along the river was more level land, reputedly the most fertile soil in Herkimer County yet the old farms were for sale, in some cases abandoned. Some of the wood-frame farmhouses stood vacant, boarded-up, but others scattered in the countryside south of Sparta were rented by drug-dealers and their girlfriends and associates. It was a shifting population of individuals not native to Herkimer County, some of whom were said to have died abrupt and mysterious deaths and their bodies buried back behind the old barns or in the woods where their bones moldered amid the tangled roots of trees.

It seemed that Magda Maria had been living in the country in one of these houses a few miles beyond the Quay Street bridge. We had not seen her on River Street in months. It was late winter.

In rehab at Watertown they pull out your guts in long twisty snarls. Entering the locked-door facility twenty-nine years old and discharged as "clean"—"sober"—five months later, weeping for my lost youth—"promise"—though the loss could've been of no more significance than crumpled and discarded trash. *We have faith in you, your talent. All that you have to live for!* Into the autumn I lived again at home like a child, regaining the weight I'd lost, a "living skeleton" I'd been when my brother had found me in the street, my muscles atrophied, my parents' love for me a burden and ridiculous like clothes I'd outgrown and eventually I fled, returned to Sparta and to River Street where not much had changed except the corner where Dunphy's had been was now a weedy parking lot. So happy to be back: almost I wanted to fall to my knees, to kiss the filthy paving stones.

In the River House there were strangers drinking in the twilit haze, more women than in the past, but none of them in any way resembled Magda Maria. Beside me was one of the Vietnam vets who'd been cheated by Ike Balboa, and he spoke now with bitter satisfaction of what had happened to Ike, the cruel bastard deserved it, and of Magda Maria it was said that she'd been injured in a fall down a flight of stairs, or left outside unconscious in the backseat of a car where she'd nearly frozen to death, but still she was alive and if she had not yet shown up at the River House she was at the Cloverleaf, or the Black Bass, or with someone at the Empire Hotel. In the Cloverleaf there was no one at the bar who resembled Magda Maria, in the Black Bass there was no one at the bar who resembled Magda Maria, except when I drew closer and stared at a woman slumped at the bar in the company of a thick-necked bald man with glinting eyeglasses suddenly I recognized Magda Maria, her beautiful face now ravaged as if corroded, her enormous eyes in shadowy sockets and her hair loose and matted falling past her shoulders not so shimmering-dark now but dull, threaded with gray. This woman was my age perhaps or older and seemed at first not to see me as I approached her staring and blinking, asked was she Magda Maria?—and now the woman took note of me, startled and uneasy but smiling, a quick mechanical smile with pursed lips as if she did not wish to bare her (stained? rotted?) front teeth. Ignoring the thick-necked bald man I asked again was she Magda Maria, and now a wary expression like a gauze mask came over her face and finally she said *Maybe. Once.*

...could die together Magda Maria whispered and the thought came to me immediate and helpless *Yes this is meant to be.* I'd brought Magda Maria back to the hotel with me, a night and a day and another night we lay together on the bed sprawling naked and heavy-limbed with sleep, the torpor of love overcame us, I loved her small white maimed feet covered in grime, the two smallest toes missing for both had had to be amputated to prevent gangrene when they froze. So lonely!— Magda Maria gripped me with her stick-arms tight around my neck, we slept, we woke, we drank from the bottle I'd brought back, Magda Maria's breasts were small and slack and her little belly protruded hard as a drum, I could feel her delicate ribs, Magda Maria was telling me a disjointed story about a rich man who'd wanted to take her to Montreal with him, and then one about her mother who'd died of a wasting-away disease a long time ago when Magda Maria had been a schoolgirl at the Catholic academy and terrified at the change in her mother, I could not follow the convolutions of Magda Maria's stories for I was so very happy in Magda Maria's arms kissing, biting,

whispering and laughing together plotting *D'you know what would be lovely?—to fall asleep with you and never wake up, just the two of us.* In our lumpy swaybacked bed with soiled sheets on the fourth floor of the Empire Hotel, naked and twined together, I tried to recall the name of Magda Maria's middle-aged lover who'd died in her arms but could only remember my envy of him.

When I was wakened hours later I could not open my eyes at first, my eyelashes were stuck together, a woman's brittle hair lay across my mouth. Magda Maria was sleeping heavily, sprawled and moaning in her sleep, sweating, tendons pulsing beneath the skin of her neck. I lay beside her in the wreckage of our love holding her as she began to breathe more laboriously, making a guttural sound *Uh-uh-uh* like a sexual moan, a taste of black bile at the back of my mouth, only a little more, I thought, another few seconds *Magda Maria I will never abandon you* but I lost consciousness and sometime in the night Magda Maria must have ceased breathing, when I awakened again she was utterly still, unyielding in my arms, her skin was clammy-cold, I could find no pulse in her throat I could find no heartbeat inside her rib-cage, in panic I called her name but I could not revive Magda Maria, I slipped from the bed and with badly shaking fingers groped for my clothes, groped for my shoes, left the darkened Room 402 of the Empire Hotel smelling of unwashed bodies, dried mucus and vomit and death, and fled.

Still she's waiting for me. In Sparta. Any time I make the

drive back. Stepping into the River House. Approaching the bar. Not the farthest end but nearer the front, near the door with the stained-glass fanlight, Magda Maria alone, with her whiskey. Waiting.

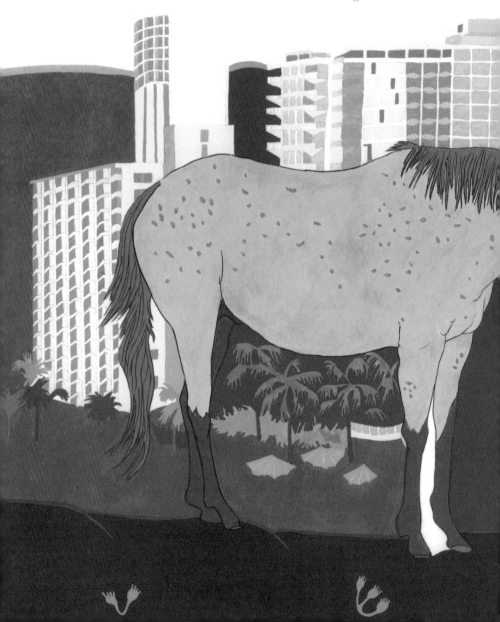

Brumby

what

THE
NAMING
OF THE
ISLANDS

David Hollander

N OW IN OUR fourth year of exile, a crew of rogues and reprobates aboard the battered carrack *Scapegrace,* we run our weary figure 8s, slicing through black water and sea foam, searching for a country of our own. Attenuated through hardships uncountable, a thousand miles from our native waters and unable to conceive of a return journey (back into the custody of our condemners, who would not likely take mercy a second time), we trip across the swollen boards, *The Scapegrace* slowly folding in upon her own brittle skeleton. We have yawed beneath towering black waves, survived the screaming violence of moonless storms and sawtooth lightning, our unskilled crew cowering beneath the yards. Lacking the initiative to strike out anew upon the deep, it is among these islands that we must find shelter, or perish. And so we circle and drop anchor, we man our shallops, plugging the holes with salvaged wads of hemp and sealing the seams with wax, and investigate these many beaches. We have never come upon the same island twice, or if we have the islands themselves have metamorphosed. Land masses jut from the sea all around us, most of them scarred and lifeless bedrock, gray-black and canted. And while most of our excursions to these various shores—*The Scapegrace* a bony silhouette at red dawn, our oars digging us to harbor—have revealed nothing but uninhabitable stone peaks and parapets, there have been exceptions both queer and redoubtable. It is these that we have determined to chronicle herein. We name these islands according to Common Law, in the assumption that we are the first examples of civilized men to have infiltrated them, however inadvertently. Our stores run low, and the crew survives on stubs of salt meat and brackish water, the occasional belt of whiskey. Exhausted and bellicose, we lay claim among these islands designed by a deranged and unhappy Creator.

FIRE

For five full days we'd sailed the shallow straits between desolate black crags, growing increasingly certain that no living thing endured this archipelago. Resentment brewed aboard *The Scapegrace* and we quarreled often, a few among us even advocating an improvident return to the open sea. It seemed that our fortunes had improved upon spotting this lonely islet in the middle distance, its shores stippled with flowering vegetation. Cheers went up and joviality briefly prevailed, the promise of food and fresh water quashing any dissent. We lowered down in parties of four, crooning a familiar chantey as we dug for shore. But soon a deathly quiet fell, punctuated only by the lonely splash of our oars.

For we had spotted the inhabitants, their skin blackened and charred, a patchwork of raw meat shining from beneath those jackets of crisp flesh. Their eyes glowed by contrast, two milk-white fishes swimming in the damaged dark. We watched them from our shallops, rowing so close to shore that when a red pyre streamed suddenly from the side of a cliff we were blistered by the heat; recoiling, we saw a wall of blue flame roar fiercely on the beach, then subside a moment later, the white sand scorched into glassy dark scoria. Combustion forced up from the island's buried heart, a place too deep—or so we ultimately decided—to be exposed by our shovels and pickaxes (for we are desperate and arrogant men, and briefly considered the prospect of dousing the flames through such an excavation, pouring casks of seawater over the swollen red interior).

Some of our crew suggest that the island floats atop a tremendous volcano, that trapped lava pushes up through the ground as if through pores in the flesh. Others—contrite men who have found their God on this voyage—insist that we have stumbled upon the gateway to the underworld, that hell itself is twenty fathoms down. They look upon the scorched and lumpen natives as one would the misshapen heretics populating the inferno. But having navigated the island's full perimeter from *The Scapegrace,* having pointed our dinghies toward all beaches, those of us in the scouting parties know better. We have seen them huddle together on a patch of recently destroyed earth, pockets of flame still sizzling in the high branches of blackened trees (which resembled nothing so much as our own sun-seared and emaciated bodies). They did not warn us away, these savages, nor react poorly to our approach. There was no tortured wailing, no gnashing of teeth. Beneath smoking boughs, dancing atop the glowing embers of scorched earth, their bare feet inured to this lesser heat, *they did not hesitate to wave us in.* They called to us in voices hoarse and broken, in a dry, reptilian language we did not recognize as human. The message, however, was clear. *It is safe to land,* their haunted eyes conveyed. *Come to us.*

We did not set foot upon their floating furnace, but watching these aborigines fry was a sport we could not deny ourselves. Our smaller boats retrieved aboard *The Scapegrace,* a half mile offshore, we enjoyed the blazes by evening, red and orange and blue, the island undergoing its terrible ablutions beneath the silver glow of a crescent moon. Dark figures ran screaming into the shallows, the scent of their cooked flesh drifting out to our salivating men. We watched a dozen of them burn that night, making hollow wagers—for what would we actually proffer up?—our mirth bubbling on the hot night air. By morning, we were gone.

BLOCK

A half day's treacherous sail through coarse channels and around rocky promontories delivered to us this uninhabited flatland. We dropped anchor and reconnoitered through a halcyon night, eager now to avoid any of the earth's dark business. Satisfied, we stepped upon the sand at dawn, extending our hands into a veil of thick green fog and stumbling blindly until the sun vaporized the noxious haze. Then we lowered our makeshift weapons and pivoted like synchronized gears in the loose yellow sand.

All around us, geometric forms rose from the earth, great blocks and spheres and pyramids of seamless design, without brick or mortar, constructed of the same pale sand from which they scaled. Sometimes three hundred feet in height, these shapes arranged themselves into the distance and obscured the horizon. We trekked on, leaving behind the silhouette of *The Scapegrace* and descending deeper into the island's interior, hoping to discover something *other,* for surely some race of fantastic mathematicians and engineers had preceded us here. Dazed and without compass, we wandered through an enormous geometry of shadows, stopping only to sip our rationed water and to chew a bit of dried fish beneath squares and rhomboids of impossible dimension. The silence was as dense as cream. No bird chirped; no breeze stirred; the sun roasted our bare backs whenever we abandoned the shade. We found nothing, of course, and by the time we thought to retreat to *The Scapegrace* dusk had arrived, and with it the same smothering fog. A few of our men (the vain and superstitious) panicked, invoking old myths of angry Gods and their maledictions, insisting that we make for our ship immediately. But without recourse to our own path, nor to sun nor constellations, we could do nothing but make camp. Fitful sleep overcame us beneath the rough walls of a tremendous rectangle, its outlines lost in the darkening haze, which grew heavier and took on the smell of smoke and rum.

In the night, whilst we dreamt of devils and beheadings, the island rearranged itself.

We had nodded off within yards of each other, but woke to find ourselves dispersed. The great rectangle no longer towered above us, though other blocks and semicircles had emerged nearby, as if the island had been renovated by a race of nocturnal giants. Scattered hundreds of yards apart, we began shouting into the warm air, slowly reconvening to find ourselves short one man, Ernest Penton, who had committed a patricide so grisly that even his peers aboard *The Scapegrace* shuddered to hear the details. The fog was beginning to burn off, and after gathering our meager possessions—a few swords, a single gunpowder matchlock loaded with pebbles, our remaining provisions—we set out after him, moving as a human wall through the remaining haze.

We found him impaled atop a great pyramid which had risen in the night, his bright blood streaming down its sides, his face turned back toward the distant ground, his innards strung from the hole in his torso like holiday streamers. He seemed about to ask us a question.

When we tried scaling the sides, hoping to retrieve him, we found them slick as ice and just as solid. We might have waited another day, allowed for the possibility of his body's return via the same silent mechanism that had rendered him airborne. Instead we abandoned his corpse with feelings of spite and envy, huffing recklessly eastward until we sighted *The Scapegrace* floating like a gargantuan oak casket, happy to welcome the moribund back upon her familiar creaking decks.

HART

A day to the south, through smaller, rocky outcroppings that none among us recognized (despite our charts, which suggest our having crossed these latitudes previously), our hopes were again stirred by a lush green island, a forest of tall trees at its center and a smooth crescent bay inviting our approach. By now the pattern was familiar, each incipient uprising aboard *The Scapegrace* ended precipitously by some new promising islet bobbing in the black. Redolent honeysuckle clung to the warm breeze as we pulled toward shore, famished but certain that here there would be meat and fresh water, that our bodies (if not our pruned souls) would be renewed. Sure enough, not fifteen feet from shore we spied a tremendous sea turtle basking in the shallows. Watson leapt into the lapping surf and grappled with the lazy monster. Two more men followed, and soon we'd slit the leathery throat and shared the warm blood from the stump of its neck, stowing the carcass in the bottom of our boat to be later roasted, carapace and all.

So satisfied were we with the blood in our bellies and thoughts of turtle meat that we did not immediately notice the drumming. But now, sated and staring into dense green brush pocked with erotic color, we bristled with awareness of a steady pounding that could mean only one thing: if we wanted this island, and already we did, we would have to take it by violence. With pointed spears and chipped shortswords, we crept from white sand into soft foliage and crooked scrub pines, their sweet-smelling sap running red from knots and twisted roots.

Huge black flies swarmed around us; the soil was dark and

rich; purple berries clung to shrubs and we chewed them greedily, surprised by the thickness of the juice that ran down our chins and necks. The unceasing drumming called us forward through brush that now grew thick and thorny, and when finally a stubborn branch caught Thompson across the bridge of his nose he swung his sword angrily into the thicket.

At once the severed branches began spouting bright red blood. Glowing, it cascaded across Thompson's bare chest and onto the black soil of the canopy floor. We will die, I am sure, with this image in our minds: vegetation spraying gore, its salty odor cutting through the fecundity of an accursed forest.

And yet what could we do but push importunately forward? Aboard *The Scapegrace* a dozen of our comrades awaited our return, starving and jaundiced, mouths ripe with rotten teeth. We lowered our blades and slid gingerly through this dense woodland. The drumming was ominously regular, *ONE-two-three, ONE-two-three*... its rhythm etched into our movements. Insects buzzed and bit; we slapped at our flesh and left their pasted carcasses there, a pox of winged viscera upon skinny sunburnt bodies. The needles shivered in the pines and the brush squeezed tighter against us, until after a time (one hour? five?) we penetrated a clearing of strange, nacreous sand, at the center of which was a small pond perhaps twenty feet in diameter.

Submerged beneath a clear, syrupy liquid—not water, but something more akin to honey in consistency—there pounded a tremendous heart, the size of three men. From beneath this fist-shaped apparatus shoots and scions ran out and into the soil, their gnarled bark throbbing. Black seams in thick bark spread with each contraction to reveal a lurid red skin. And then one of us—Aiden Hart, who in our homeland had brutally raped and murdered a seamstress—took his spear and pushed it through that clarified honey, gently piercing this enormous, pulsing organ which, puckering, released a stream of bubbles into its liquid amnion.

The percussive tempo increased immediately, that same *ONE-two-three* but in double time now, and higher in pitch. We stood perfectly still. A moment passed. And another. A fly landed silently on Watson's forehead. And then the entire island began to hemorrhage.

We spun and ran. All around us, leaves and pods began to explode, making small hissing noises and spraying thick heliotrope liquid into the air. Pine needles emitted a fiery drizzle as we sprinted through thornbushes, swinging our swords indiscriminately now, rampaging through fountains of blood, a high sun baking it to our burnt skins, the pungency of slaughtered hogs hanging ripe in the hot, wet air. There were men among us screaming, if I recall correctly, and the island trembled as if built upon an uncertain foundation.

Our shallop awaited us, the turtle's carcass a quainter form of butchery, its severed head's dead eyes chronicling our departure into water stained violet, the dye running out in an immense cloud, the island dying in our wake. Rowing away, we watched it happen: trees reduced to crisp yellow husks, vegetation crumbling to black ash, black soil bleached pale as the living island bled out. After a moment, we remembered the turtle, and our thoughts turned to whether or not we were responsible for sharing this meager sustenance with those left behind on *The Scapegrace,* which we approached as if from the most wicked of battles, painted in the colors of warfare and massacre.

ABOARD

By now the decks of our carrack simmer with violence. Hungry pugilists swing tumid fists and we all take sides, eager for blood. None among us can countenance a return to the sea, but those who had once advocated such a course now openly vow murder upon those responsible for our vagaries among these dire straits. The astrolabe was found destroyed yesterday at dawn, the celestial bodies chiseled from its face and the device entire nailed to the foremast. A futile act of protest, or else crude misanthropic humor. This log is now kept fast and secreted from harm; it is our last precious connection to the realm whose liberties we squandered. Nights pass beneath a waning sulfur moon and our desiccated bodies give out one by withered one. And yet the Almighty toys with us. Just as weapons are drawn aboard our creaking decks, just as men declare their blood pacts with parched and swollen tongues, we sight some previously undiscoverable bit of earth. It is as if these islets were humps on the spine of an enormous serpent that rolled lazily near the surface, renewing our dimwitted hopes before descending again into the drink. But must every island mete out some new variety of punishment? Can there not be that one upon whose shores even such men as these might find redemption? We lower down again and again, in search of that single palatable fate.

RAT

More rock than island, this craggy mound of feldspar glinted and shimmied from a distance of two miles, persuading us to turn the bow of our sluggish and beloved carrack and make cautiously for the reflected light. Riding a deep sluice of black water, the smell of sulfur rising, we drifted to within two hundred yards. We lowered a boat and rowed to within a stone's throw, only to confirm the supposed illusion: this rocky wafer—barely larger than our own *Scapegrace*—was covered in them. Rats. They swarmed over every inch of ground, their skins like hot tar, ten thousand oily rodents with pink tails swinging serpentine. On this stony hummock they fornicated with and devoured one another (as if these acts were synonymous), twin-chisel teeth tearing madly into the pink flesh of a lover, a child, a parent. A frenzied mass of sex and carnage, blood and semen, writhing on mounds of their own ripe excrement, the testicles of the larger males dangling like dark plums.

We did not land, but we approached the pernicious shoreline, reaching out to snatch two dozen of the little demons, risking fingers and suffering filthy puncture wounds, whipping them by unctuous tails against the shallop's pine boards. And then we rowed back with our eldritch cargo, Thompson vomiting over the side, though with our shrunken stomachs even the bile has dried up, so that he wretched a sort of yellow ash.

But this meal of rat meat cut our hunger and delivered another tentative peace. We gutted them on the decks of *The Scapegrace,* roasted them whole. We devoured them down to the bones, which we chewed on for days, sucking at the greasy pink marrow that tasted like sweat and treacle, surprisingly sweet. We have tried in vain to return to Rat Island, to feast again on this bounty. Alas—it, too, has disappeared.

THE TWINS

Not three full days ago, we sailed through a shallow breech between identical islands, their silver shores tapered down from low green hills, mirror images of fecundity. And yet we know well enough to distrust these first giddy impressions. Our bodies wasted down to kindling (just that day our numbers dwindled to ten, as two more succumbed to starvation accelerated by enteric disease, their corpses still warm and flushed with fever hours after their passing, when we dumped them over the side), we flipped a coin stamped with our beloved monarch's image to choose between islands, and the five strongest among our fast-expiring crew lowered down and dug in. We beached the shallop in soft sand, hopping barefoot upon the island, our bodies pocked with pink sores and blue bruises.

Once on land, we immediately took to halfhearted quarreling. Should we seek out the island's fresh water, our fundamental commodity, of which we had but a few days' supply remaining? Or should we concentrate our efforts on food, the gathering of roots and berries, or the possible (though unlikely) discovery of jungle boar rippling with muscle?

As we bickered, swollen bees zipped by like striped bits of pastry, an emerald forest one hundred yards inland exuding humidity like a sweet liqueur. Watson was the first to identify the rustling in the branches. We noticed him staring into the greenery, and one by one we shut our mouths and joined him in scrutiny. A moment later a call went up, too loud and too shrill to be the voice of any shorebird. The arrows followed, a hundred or more, soaring from the forest in a slow, high arc, and then emerging just behind them a phalanx of painted aborigines, their spears piercing the warm air, their war cries cleaving the hazy sunlight, a verdict of sorts. We had found our cannibals.

In a harried dance we dodged the lazy arrows, all of us but Watson. His thigh skewered, he dropped to the beach, a thin fountain of blood erupting from the wound as the rest of us boarded the shallop and pushed off. Ah, Watson! He tried to rise, his wasted body all wire and parchment. We watched them overtake him as we pulled wildly at our oars, unprepared after all for true warfare, made fainthearted by our more private battles with dysentery, intestinal flu, scurvy, and sea fever. The savages enveloped him like ants dismantling a piece of gristle.

We did not set out immediately for *The Scapegrace*, however. The four of us made instead for the second island, drifting beneath the shadow of our carrack's bow (where no man stood watch). Already the ordeal seemed unreal to us, resembling as it did the architecture of our many fevered dreams.

Still, when we found his body—on the *second* island—his face half-eaten, his limbs severed and strewn about, his trunk eviscerated, our cowardice was as palpable as a furry moth. He stared at us through enormous eyes, his serpent tattoo the clearest indicator that it was in fact our shipmate, Watson. From where we stood, the first island was a yellow hump in the middle distance. Fearful of the savages' return, we loaded the carcass piece by bloody piece into the shallop, figuring burial at sea was the least we could offer one of our own. Before pushing off, Hart could not help but perform the simplest of experiments. He raised his hackbut toward the sky and pulled the matchlock, firing its single shot. Sure enough, a second powder blast could be clearly heard, an instant later, from the other island, where a tiny puff of smoke drifted upward. Another set of ourselves stood there, performing this same experiment, feeling as we did that theirs was the power of autonomy, and that these men across the channel were mere reflections, shadows, phantom twins risen from mysterious ether.

ADRIFT

Rowing back for *The Scapegrace* we descried our doubles returning from *their* island, and some strange conflux seemed all but assured. But the nearer we approached, the less substantial their forms became, dissipating into the same ether from which they had congealed. Not even the ripple of their oars survived our arrival alongside our carrack, which we boarded with eerie suspicions regarding our own solidity. Watson's blood stained our flesh and we felt certain that we were being watched, aware not only of our vanished twins but also of their own invisible *Scapegrace* which endured some uncanny permutation of our fruitless odyssey.

We have since spotted, in the near distance, a long, flat island whose barrier beach displays a sunken forest of scrub pines. Toward this next inevitability we creep, with tattered sails clutching at a slight easterly breeze and our carrack moaning, seemingly chagrined. Above deck the last of our fevered crew debate the surest channel through treacherous shallows, their rusting weapons at the ready, would-be malcontents and mutineers but shipmates above all else, bound together by fate and by character. Does suffering in one precinct of the cosmos alleviate the burden elsewhere? Is there a single Almighty, or rather a multitude thereof, each working in mad isolation on His own dubious project? This chronicle exists under lock in the ship's binnacle, and also in the minds of a thousand doppelgängers, whose more fortunate destinies exist, unwritten, in the recesses of my own internal seascape. Momentarily, we pull again for shore.

Alter-Real

THE
APE MAN

ALEXANDER MacBride

T_____'s FOSTER MOTHER—do you know this story? His foster mother (an ape, of course) had just lost her baby—lost it in the sense that it had died, because she was actually still carrying the little body around—it had lost its grip on her fur when she was running away from something, the bull ape, I think, and fallen down out of the trees, dozens of feet. Smashed practically to pieces, poor sweet little thing.

But so it wasn't very long after that that the apes smashed their way into the little house where T_____'s parents lived—where T_____ himself lived, for that matter, because he was just about a year old at that time. Now, his mother had just died the night before, quietly, after a long illness, and the father was sitting at his little desk in despair, and the baby, that being T_____, was lying there in his little crib, crying for his mother—the mother who was lying there dead in her bed, poor woman, just as the father had found her except that he had pulled the sheet over her face.

And so the apes smashed their way in, and the big bull ape, I don't remember his name, pulverized the father, just mangled him, poor man, but before the bull ape could grab little T_____

from his crib and squeeze him to a pulp or bite out his tiny guts the ape-mother, the one whose baby had just died, rushed forward and snatched him up and dropped her own dead ape-baby in his place in the crib. And then she dashed out hooting and climbed up to the top of a tree, out of the bull ape's reach, and waited there until it was safe, waited with her new little baby, who wasn't called T_____ at that time, of course, but who got that name eventually among the apes. And from that time forward the ape-mother raised him as an ape-baby, and he grew as an ape, and lived as an ape, and came to be first among all the apes. And we all know that story. I have just remembered that the ape-mother was named Kala.

But of course there was also the ape-baby, the dead ape-baby, left in the crib, left in the little house when the other apes ran off, left there with the dead mother and the dead father. And just as you would expect, just as the ape-mother loved the little human baby, the dead-mother and the dead-father loved the little dead ape-baby, the little ape-baby that death had stolen from his mother, that they had been given in place of their own little live baby, whom the ape-mother had stolen from them. And the dead-mother and the dead-father raised the little dead ape as the dead do, as a dead person, and he grew as a dead person and lived as a dead person and came to be first among all the dead, just as T_____, who I suppose amounts to his brother, in a way, came to be first among the apes; just as T_____, the little living human boy, became Lord of the Apes, the little dead ape boy became Lord of the Dead. And just as T_____ eventually moved on to less archetypal activities, Opar and such, his brother, who these days we call the Ape-Man, moved on to a more ambiguous situation, out among others, out in the world, where you and I are. He's dead, of course, but being dead has never been a straightforward matter, and the things a dead person can do and the things a living person can do are in many respects the same things. And the Ape-Man has done many things.

It's been decades since T_____ died, grew very old and died, but the Ape-Man, being already dead from the beginning, is still with us, is still alive, in a way. He is always far away, standing back behind almost everything; they say there is no evil he does not have his hand in, or his finger at the very least. And T_____ was not that way of course, he was always good, but he and the Ape-Man were never enemies. Each held all the other's grief; at being dead, on the one hand, and on the other, at being alive.

Of course, there is no doubt that he is a terrible creature, and our enemy to the very last day of the world. I would never say that he is not. But I hope you will remember that once he was a tiny much-beloved little thing, a poor little dead thing, a little dead ape loved by his mother and then loved by the human dead, loved twice over. We will never be rid of him, but that thought may console us.

Mustang

what

PEACE-
KEEPERS,
1995

Kenneth Bonert

IN THE MORNING they flew in on a Hercules and landed in Zagreb. A corporal picked Henry up and took him through the center of town for his accreditation at the UN building. Outside stood a line of painted bricks with photographs and lit candles and mourning hooded women with placards.

They crossed the border before noon and were in the green mountains by midafternoon. Henry, a bony and inelegant man with a pointing Adam's apple, sat quietly. He saw a castle through the blurring trees, poised and medieval over a gorge, perfectly genuine but for a stone wall newly caked with the blue paint of an immense Bosniak flag.

Later on he saw bomb craters and spring flowers. Villages with blackened walls and gaping spaces for roofs like great mouths calling out in perpetuity to a sky so silken it shone down like an inverted lake of brightest lacquer. In towns there were mosques reduced to piles of ashen dust akin to ground bone, topped often with the lopsided spire of a fallen minaret. Graffiti lay on wreckage everywhere. But in the forested countryside they crossed narrow bridges over bright waters, clear and twinkling in the stony shallows beneath. The air was nimble and clean and the sun washed through the verdant filter of the enclosing woods in great crystalline beams of shattering purity.

It was only after two hours of silence that the driver began to speak. His name was Pigeon and he had a bubble face and caramel skin, a hairline of oddly meandering stubble. His nose was flat and wide and his accent was untraceable though its methodical tempo held some certain essence of Indian as Henry knew Indian, the Cree of his childhood in north Quebec, that shrewd consideration given each phrase, as if words were coins and conversations gaming tables.

—Tell you something, Pigeon said. I never met a reporter in my life.

—Well. I've never been in a war zone myself.

—Where you from guy?

—Montreal.

—Montreal. What you report in Montreal?

—Last thing I wrote, let's see. A drunk killed two people but I couldn't say he was drunk.

—No?

—Wasn't allowed.

—Allowed by who.

—Ask my editor. Ask who this drunk was and who bought how much advertising a year.

—Man.

There was some quiet.

—It's who controls the media, Pigeon said. Henry looked

at him but there was nothing more. And no more talk for some miles. The jeep wound through the green hills. Henry could not believe the rolling beauty between the ruined villages. He thought of Vermont and then the summer hills of Tennessee but neither was perfectly apt. There was a Central European density here, blacker trunks and a feeling of gloom and moisture to the air even on this most dry and unclouded of days. As if human history had in its immense trampling inflicted some tragic manner of subvisible bruising on all things.

—Wish I could have written the truth, Henry said. The only thing I ever wanted to do was write the truth. But they don't let you. You think the truth is such a simple easy thing to tell. If it happened it happened and put it down. If not then not. See it and write it. I saw the drunk and the family of the dead in the lobby of the court when they met the first time. He was crying like a child and then his lawyer took him away. Week after the verdict I saw him again. Downing vodka doubles in a peeler bar. When I left there was his new Corvette in the lot.

—How about that.

The drive broke at Velika Kladuša, where the Canadians had a base on what seemed to Henry to be a stone quarry, for all was exposed rock or crushed white shale like the landscape of some fallen moon and fine albino grit seeped into the edges of the eyes. They went on almost immediately. Now when the woodland shadows lengthened they were close to the river Una, a strident current with a minted glassy surface. And Henry had his first long look at the people of the region: horse-and-carts, wheeze trucks, pitchforks, women with bundled heads or sometimes shocks of blond hair like new straw, workingmen without jeans.

—Soil looks rich here, Henry remarked. So black.

—Yes.

—They farm here.

—Farm. Kill. Plant the bodies. Grow the harvest with the blood for food and eat it down again, blood into blood.

Henry looked to see if Corporal Pigeon was smiling but the strange bubble face with its wide nose and awkward hairline was calm and sincere, pointed square and steady at the windshield.

It was dusk when they reached the town of Ključ. Garbage was being burned in a long smear by the river, raising a sweetsickly waft. The base was on the far side of a tunnel bored through the crust of a mountain. On the facing slopes stood wasted homes, some still with their slanted redtile roofs or portions thereof, most without, the concrete walls pale and vacant, so stark against the fading sky, like the planted bones of giants.

It wasn't until the following afternoon that he saw Corporal Pigeon again. He was in an armored personnel carrier Henry joined, one of several in a routine patrol. Henry wore a navy flak jacket and a camera round the neck. He sensed Pigeon watching him from below as he rode halfway out the hatch, shooting photos past the shoulders of the forward gunner. When at last he sank back, flushed and windscrubbed, Pigeon touched his shoulder.

—Where's your helmet at?

—My what?

They were shouting over the engine grind.

—Hel-met

—No one gave me one, Henry said.

Pigeon shook his head. —No one even cares.

—What?

—You know what's out there. Do you?

Henry watched him.

—Listen guy. Me to you, you need a helmet boy. You tell them, those officers I seen with you, tell them get me one.

—Baker and Lacroix.

—Captains.

—Yeh.

—Well no captain ever had to clean a mess of brains off of a Bison.

Henry looked at the steel walls around them. —This's a Bison right.

—This is a Bison.

—What are you saying?

—What the hell else they tell you?

—Nothing.

—I seen you up there. You better start waving, guy. I'm serious.

—Waving.

—And smiling. I'm serious.

—You're serious.

—Don't look at me all like that. They should have told you. Make you realize the snipers and the hostility. As a new face you have got to come across friendly to these folks. I would go so far to say there is nothing more important you can do for your safety right now. Those captains haven't been here maybe a week themselves.

—I believe you.

—You damn should. This my third tour. They should have instructed you that smile and wave is number one.

—All right. Thanks.

—So they can get used to who you are. The Bosniak corps, out there and watching.

Henry nodded and started up. Pigeon caught his sleeve. —They told you the one thing what never to do right.

Henry frowned.

—Jesus, Pigeon said. Listen. When you do wave don't show a full hand to them, whatever else. These are Muslim people, believers and mountain folk. They have their particular ways. A full hand, now that is a deadly insult. Polite thing, do it like this. He folded the two last fingers to the open palm. Henry watched.

—I'm serious, Pigeon said.

—I can see you are.

Henry aped the wave.

—I'm only telling you.

—Thanks man.

—You can ask anyone.

—No, no, Henry said. I appreciate. Thank you. I do appreciate.

The sun enlarged. The morning waned. Came a threshold shift

in the quality of the light: a cloying redness draped about the shape of things like a toxic veil and the air turned parched as dust. Henry baked and dripped inside his flak jacket and denims; yet he kept his grin alive.

He waved down over the camouflage armor, at women in kerchiefs lugging bundles in file, at big-eyed children with crammed fingers between their teeth. After each wave he raised his Pentax, aimed with care, shot them all. The engine roared and the carrier ascended. Winding roads grooved like bolt threads into the slopes. The radio antennae flopping like a marine animal. In rougher sections Henry let himself loll back. He was okay, he told himself, waving to the peasants, often with both hands, his three-digit signals wideflung over his head.

It hardly bothered him that they didn't wave back. Persistence was an ingrained virtue, a reporter's virtue. Occasionally the people below looked back up at him and his wide gesticulations with their steady black eyes, unblinking, less often with irises of emerald green. Occasionally their mouths worked. Peasant folk, he thought. Earth salt. Not easily won, which only made him shake his threefinger flags and white North American teeth that much the harder.

After a while he believed he could feel the meager dry air thinning as they climbed. The falling beams of red light arced from above were the tips of long solar claws; they dug into the flesh of his scalp, the meat of his cheeks. He wished he'd packed sunscreen but he'd neglected even a cap on this ride, reckoning on the brim getting in the way of his shooting.

Finally the Bison left the road at a large meadow. Several other vehicles like it were already drawn up. Farther out there were troops lying on their bellies in the short grass, firing rifles at distant white boards. When the engine shut off Henry could hear them—it was only a gentle popping sound on the wind. In the farther distance the woodsy hillsides resumed, looking green and cool as a mineral lake under the relentless sun.

Pigeon was helping unload armament. Taking a knee, Henry squeezed off shots of the vehicles then dug out his notebook and shorthanded some details for the cutline. *Royal Canadian Dragoons, Squadron A. Bisons parked in formation above the Sanica Valley.* He shot more and wrote: *IFOR Bison markings = Implementation Force, ref implem Dayton Accords.*

Bison, he thought. How we crave the wildness our grandfolks snuffed. Name our weapons for those butchered by their like. Nice. Bloodier chutzpah there never was.

He shot close-ups of the soldiers on their bellies. The heat so sapped him that at moments he also wanted to lie down in the grass, to close his eyes. The heat made the hillsides unbuckle from the earthly firmament and float and waver like banners in a tunnel of testing winds. He was interviewing a soldier who looked too young to shave when Pigeon interrupted. —Don't be no virgin in a whorehouse, guy. He held out a C8 carbine. Henry shook his head. The young soldier had used the break to drift gratefully away.

—Thought you supposed to be into truth, Pigeon said. He racked the weapon, beckoned. Henry found himself following through the dreamish burning air; everything felt so muted and distant under the swatting press of the heat on the land.

In the rear of the vehicles Pigeon flung out a beret on the grass. —One of theirs, he said. Now grease that spider. Zip his mongrel guts.

—No, Henry said, twisting from the weapon. No thank you.

—I seen your eyes. You want to. Righteous killer eyes. He spun and fired a burst. The fabric jumped. Again he held the weapon out to Henry. This time Henry's hand rose.

—Yes, Pigeon said, and let go. Henry had to grasp it to stop it falling. The rifle was ludicrously light, like a child's toy. For some reason this depressed him. Pigeon turned aside and swept his arm at the beret. —Be an angel of death, he said. Make some dirty hell.

Henry's face throbbed. He hesitated. —Go ahead, Pigeon told him.

A voice barked from behind. They both turned to watch the patrol leader, a Sergeant Hanron, striding across. —Fuck's this now, Pigeon?

—Press tour, Sarge.

Hanron looked Henry up and down.

—He's okay, Sarge, Pigeon said.

—There's no rounds for this bullshit.

—That's too bad, Pigeon softly said, his quick dark eyes flicking between the sergeant and Henry.

—Make that weapon safe, soldier.

—Sir.

Henry handed the C8 back, feeling sheepish and guilty.

—Sorry eh, Hanron told him.

—No problem, Henry said.

Hanron sniffed and seemed embarrassed. —But you got good shots out here...

—Oh yeah.

He shrugged. —Well.

—Hey Sarge, Pigeon said.

—What now.

—I was thinking swingtown, Pigeon said, ducking his head toward Henry.

—Shut up now, Hanron said, grimacing.

—He's okay, Pigeon said. Not like them others.

Hanron stared at him. He was stocky and ginger-haired, with a wirebrush mustache and terrier eyes. —Corporal, I told you make that fucking weapon safe.

—Sir.

—And get it stowed. Double time.

—Sir.

Pigeon pulled the C8's magazine, worked the bolt and looked up the breech, then moved off, treading lightly on the stub of his own noon shadow.

Hanron sighed. —Always one thing or another, that guy. Chee-rist.

Henry tried to smile then found himself crumpling down into a squat. Hanron leaned over. —You sick?

—No. Just tired. The heat...

—Look, I can take you but I need a absolute promise before Jesus.

—What?

Hanron sank down beside him. —For keeping this a hundred percent to yourself is what. I'll show you for you but not as any reporter. That clear?

—Yes fine, Henry said. For me.

Hanron put out his hand and Henry shook it.

—So long as we are clear.

When the Bisons moved out again, Henry went with Sergeant Hanron's. Soon, unhelmeted, he was up in the hatch giving his three-digit wave and numb smile down to a family on a cart behind a horse as they passed them. An old man was supine in the back, with a face like crumpled parchment, a few wildly spoking yellow teeth left in the black gash of the gums. He lifted his stick arm and pointed directly at Henry with a withered finger and began to say things in his language, audible even over the Bison's roar. Henry's headache was evolving. He reeled a bit. Abruptly, he was neither smiling nor waving and didn't care. A woman at the front of the cart twisted around and spoke to the old man and tried to push the stick arm down but it stayed pointed at Henry and the ancient mouth kept moving until the cart had fallen away around the bend behind.

Strange, Henry thought. Everything so strange. These hills, these roads—they were a world-war documentary come to life.

He was penetrating black-and-white footage he'd long since absorbed: a landscape so long internal kept on steadily blooming into technicolor around him, as if brushed over softly with a vivifying magic. But it was life, he kept telling himself, this, here, now, all. The moving present. A trap of moments. It struck him he might have been a German officer riding a Panzer and the old man in the cart must have seen just such a man on just such a pass, with this sun overhead, exactly thus. Foreign diesel and steel roaring in his mountains.

He blinked and found himself receiving a revelation, unsayable and profound. Straining to pull this sudden insight down into clear words in his mind, he lost his physical balance and banged his chin, saw dark shimmer-edged abrasions burrowing like harried worms across the surface of his view of things. They twinkled and cleared. He lowered himself back into the sauna shade inside the steel and found a reasonably stable corner and hunkered. The radio crisped and babbled and Hanron kept shouting things into his headset. He was diverting their vehicle from the convoy.

When they stopped again, it was opposite a knoll past a stream of milky crystal and then a rock face and a few spare lone trees. From the branches corpses hung. Fat black birds were eating of them. A wind blew gently and these cold upside-down former people hanging before Henry were stirred as he watched, strung on wires like the obscene blood fruits of some devil orchard beyond all mortal reckoning, the gruesome rubbing chimes of bonebitten rust wires scratching bark carrying back across the pellucid air to where he stood and stood and continued to.

—Why we called it swingtown you can see.

Henry couldn't think.

The fat birds were beaking at the putrid swollen things. He licked his rasping lips with his parched tongue. The birds didn't seem to be in any kind of a rush. There was a busily writhing halo of black insects. The bodies hanging from the wires were all puffed out, stiffly discolored, like vast condoms crammed with anthracite coal, even the trailing limbs, even the massively protuberant tongues below the swaying heads.

—Now why, Henry was saying. Why…

—Whoa whoa whoa there, Hanron called. You crazy?

—Sorry, Henry said. Sorry, I forgot.

—There's no forget. You stay on the road. On the damn roads. Am I using English? Do you like having legs?

—I'm sorry.

—Don't be sorry to me. Remember where in the hell it is that you are man.

—Sorry.

—Shit dammit.

Henry came back to the road, still trying to understand how he had drifted out onto the gravel slope. What untold manner of force had called out to his limbs, that they might begin of their own volition to creep themselves nearer the fascination that held his eyes and mind as steadily as a nightbeam on a cudding elk's. What secret ring of gravity. What call of death.

Then they stood there, just looking. Henry may have swayed slightly.

Hanron pointed high. —The Dayton line just up here. The Serbs over top. Imamovic's men say it's Serbs did it but the Serbs say it's Bosniaks. We say if not for anything but hygiene get it together and clean up. But there it is. Back and forth and bullshit. Watch it fall on us in the end.

—Imamovic. Who's Imamovic?

—Bosniak commander. This sector's all his corps of irregulars in charge. Muslim neighborhood which they got back after the Croats busted out, the big offensive last spring. Every place here has its warlord runs things. Imamovic is the man here, capital em. King of the mountain Muslims. Sometimes they call him The Haji.

—You think he did this. His guys.

Hanron sniffed. —Aw shit, never stops. He took off his sunglasses and peered frankly into Henry's face. Better get yourself a hat buddy. You look ready to keel.

Henry nodded and turned back to the Bison.

—Hey.

—Yeah?

—So long as we both are absolutely clear.

—Never saw one thing.

Later in the mess at the base Henry had dinner with captains Lacroix and Baker. He dipped a paper napkin in his water cup and mopped his face. —Christ Jesus, he said. His forehead felt a size too small and five degrees too hot. Lower down, he was shaking and increasingly bilious. The nausea came in tiny peaking waves.

—You look, Baker told him, like a Gaspé lobster I once boiled. Shiny, red, and near death.

—Thanks.

—It is unholy, Lacroix said.

—Thanks.

—Not'all, Baker said. He was eating small cheeses with a knife and a fork and great concentration. His long sleeves were rolled down to the wrists and properly buttoned and he had a serviette tucked into his collarfront. He was a sometimes amusing Englishman who'd transported himself to Toronto in the seventies, an actuary by trade, and a reserve officer in the Canadian forces for which reason Henry could not approach fathoming. Both Baker and Lacroix were media escort officers—arbitrary authority figures already grown profoundly oppressive and commensurately irritating to Henry's laboring spirit.

Henry asked if either of them knew of Pigeon.

Baker, it seemed, could chew and swallow without needing to move his chin in any significant way. —Corporal who now?

—Pigeon. Fetched me in Zagreb. And he was out on the patrol today.

—Never heard of him.

—Sort of odd.

—Oh yes?

—Somewhat.

Baker looked up. —Henry.

—Yes.

—Henry. Mate.

—Yes.

—Don't let yourself get too socialized.

Henry would have smiled but lacked the requisite motivation.

But Baker, earnest, had leant forward. —Best to get your quotes and get out. The men. These downhomers, they're mostly scum of the Newfie east and whatnot. It's army or it's federal pen. One eyebrow bent stiffly upward. He added: A nebulous thatch into which reporters must blithely wander.

—What?

—Dinna worry. We'll keep you safe.

Lacroix was murmuring, his eyes elsewhere. —Hello my sweetness, my dove and my light.

Henry looked up and a striking uniformed woman with long black hair was approaching.

—That's Sonya, Baker said. A civvie. Unit translator.

Presently she was saying hi. She looked at Henry. Then Lacroix asked her to marry him. She threw back her head, her laugh almost decadent in its blaring, like an abrupt expression of climax. Henry, looking into the creamy tube of her exposed throat, was stirred. —Are you Muslim?

Sonya's smile flickered but held. Baker took his spell at issuing tutting noises as Lacroix had but pitched his with more severity. Lacroix was clearing his throat hard. She said: —My father was Serbian, Mama is half-Croatian half-Bosnian, so...

Henry found sounds preforming in his mouth felt mooshy to the tongue, unready. He sought greater control of the lips with the aid of his hand.

Meanwhile Sonya looked at Baker then to Lacroix, who told her: —He's just in.

—Our new boy, Baker said.

—You feel okay? she said.

Henry almost shook his head but marshalled himself for a nod, and: —Tell me something. I want to know what you think.

—Yes.

—Whose fault is it. This.

—Oh God, Lacroix said.

Baker said: —Eat your spaghetti now, Henry, there's a good man.

—I mean all of it, Henry said. He moved his hands helplessly.

Sonya shrugged; her bottom lip came out. —Vot, she said, it's vur, it is vur, that's all. To get answer it depends on who it is you talk with. So you hev to ask a lot questions. Talk a lot of people. So.

Another shrug. She looked back over her shoulder. —Bye guys.

—Don't leave us darling, Lacroix said.

—You two are laugh for me.

—No, no, Baker said.

—Just look, Sonya said, shaking her tough smile.

—Sonya, Henry said.

—Careful for the sun, she said.

She touched her cheek. —So red.

—Yet another commie, Baker said.

—You should go see doctor, Sonya said. You should lied down.

A last smile then she'd turned then was walking away.

Lacroix groaned. —I'll lied down my face on your magnificent tits. Anytime.

Baker spluttered. He turned to Henry: —I think she likes you, despite your grotesque lack of tact.

—I'm married, Henry lied, not feeling like raising the topic of bitter divorce and its inevitably related subject, the fearsome psychic blight of temporary misogyny.

—Tact for a reporter, Lacroix said. Please.

—Well why not, Baker said.

—Oh please. Lacroix swatted some air down, grimacing.

Henry sighed. —You try to figure it all out. For yourself.

Both captains laughed, heartily.

—Oh please oh please, Lacroix said.

Henry dabbed at his hot face with a wetted napkin again. A shiver rose in his bowels and his skin prickled.

—Did you hear the lady, Baker was saying. Little doodad called war. A portion of the human condition and always will be.

—They all got along here, Henry said. No one could tell them apart. And just one day? Wake up and what.

The laughter kept spilling from both in near-equal measure now. I am not abashed, Henry thought. I am not. I refuse to be. He set his teeth and shivered.

—You make us weepy, Baker said, thou keeper of the true liberal faith.

—Oh he's not political, Lacroix said. He's just hurt.

Baker made a wry twist of his thin mouth and Henry considered that Lacroix, chubby and unblessed with a face as bland

and gray as unseasoned oatmeal, was hardly what he appeared to be. There were brighter vulpine elements buried in the soft eyes. A thing to bear in mind. He was a career naval officer and carried the rank of lieutenant, based out of Esquimalt on Vancouver Island.

—Maybe it's simply history, Henry said. An excess of history.

—My friend, Baker said, I'll take consciousness over animal reflex any day. The past is the great informer that allows being human as a possibility.

—Well then maybe it's not, Henry heard his voice say.

—Not what.

—Human.

They looked at him, unlaughing both. Henry set his teeth and shivered. His mind over his buried shivering was full of black death in the hissing trees. Then that shattering feeling he'd had in the Bison on the arcing track. He tried to find a phrase at the least from that enigmatic gut thought, that glimmer. A word.

—Maybe there's a thing, he said. Something unnameable. Alive in the mountains. Eternal.

—Oh he has a name all right. And he's quite mortal, pal.

Lacroix shook his head subtly at Baker.

Catching this covert spark of communication between them, Henry spoke: —Oh I've heard of Imamovic.

Baker smiled too lightly. —Bravo. Join the hordes.

—What have you heard? Lacroix asked.

—A thing or two.

—You know he was a carpenter? Before the war.

—Yes, Henry lied. Of course.

—And now, Lacroix said, turning to Baker, at ten grand a week from us alone...

—Uh uh uh, Baker quickly said, his look compressed to a ray of heavy-browed concern.

Not in front of the surly kid, Henry thought, welling with bitterness. Screw you all. He reached for his dessert and held his peace.

In the last of the evening's illumination, Henry had a formal tour of Camp Spruce Willow. Lovely name, he thought. Perhaps it had been calculated to arouse in the Canadian minds of its inhabitants resplendent images of cool northern forests and sparkling lakes, canoe trips and the peaceful ache of childhood nostalgia for summer camp holidays long slipped by.

What Henry saw in Camp Spruce Willow was a blasted hollowed concrete hulk, three stories high, whose clanking innards had once excreted slabs of gray carpet for the Soviet bloc. The factory machines were stacked to one side now, cobwebbed and rusting. The Royal Dragoons were bedded down on the vast floorspace instead, under canvas in separate tents.

Outside it was all concrete dust and razor wire. Some men played an angry scuffing game of soccer behind the shower tent.

—Basically it was Serbs holed up under fire, Staff Sergeant Lucas said. She was from the base commander's office and she wore horn-rimmed glasses and her plain irritation. Our engineers got in here they found dead animals and human shit.

—Shit?

She looked at him over her glasses. —Gallons. And some of their dead unburied. Don't put that in.

—Of course. He smiled over his scribbling.

—The stink and the disease risk. They wore gas masks while cleaning and said you could not believe human beings were capable. She looked away.

—A hell hole, Henry said.

—Home sweet whatever.

Henry took a step and looked back past her at the risible pale edifice, its high empty panes and interior gloom. —I look at it and think There stands the Soviet Union, he said. There she is. The whole story, written truly in concrete dust and all anyone needs to ask or ever know.

She squinted at him like an examining doctor. —Uh huh.

—Well. Thanks.

—No problem. You're done, right.

He nodded and they started back.

—Oh and I meant to ask one other thing, he said. I was told you're the one who should give me the exact figure of the rent?

She stopped to squint again. —Rent?

—Yip. I think they said it was ten thousand?

—They. Who's this they?

—Jeez I forget. But it's true right. Not a huge detail but.

She looked off, put some hair behind one ear. —I'm not sure what you mean. Saying this warily.

He knew from experience what he had to do here was to wait.

But when she turned back he could see it wasn't going to fly.
—I wouldn't know.
—You're base commander's office, right? All my base questions?
—I have no idea about any rent.
—You sure?
She withered him with a measure of silent disdain. Then:
—You're getting into stuff that is way above my pay scale.
Maybe yours too. Understand?
He nodded.

Henry took a shower in the ablutions tent with black rubber mats
underfoot and blasting nozzles all around and a constant inflow
and egress of naked men, many of whom howled and strutted.
Directed afterward to the upright plastic toilet stalls, commonly
called jack shacks in honor of their masturbatory function, he
couldn't see how the stench in the days of a Serbian occupation
could have ever been appreciably worse, gallons or no. He crapped
gingerly, resting his weight on his palms, shivering. He was
diarrheic and his guts roiled and pained him like knives. He
finished and his eyelids drooped.

Entering his little tent he flung himself down onto the
stretcher, pulled a pillow over his head to blunt the ambient
murmuring and electric light, then dropped off precipitously
into a steep black well of utter sleep. In his dream he was in a
hardwood forest enclosed in soft rain. Then something reached
out and clasped his shoulder from behind. He jerked spastically.

—Henry. Henry.

—Aw gewway, gewway.

—Henry. Hey.

—Lee me.

—Henry wake up.

—Fuck. Shit.

—Come on, sit up.

—I'm. Ah. God. What?

—It's Captain Lacroix, Henry. Captain Baker too. Sit up. Here we go.

—Jesus. You guys. I just. I just lay down. A minute.

—It's a little after midnight. We thought we should wake you, Baker said.

—It's important, Lacroix said.

A blurry Baker held out a white thing from which scented steam curled.

—You might want to get that down you, Lacroix said.

—Don't want coffee. Sleep.

—You've got to wake up, Lacroix said.

Henry scrubbed his hot face and looked up at them, blinking.

—There's this problem, Lacroix said.

—So some would most certainly say, Baker said. The flavored moist heat of the coffee steam was not agreeable to Henry. He pushed it away, a styrofoam cup, just that, nothing sinister. Baker set it down softly on the concrete.

—You guys, Henry said. He rolled slowly up, groaning, and put his feet on the ground. After a moment, working very slowly, he removed his shoes and socks.

—This is serious, Lacroix said.

Henry studied the captains through his crimped eyes. Neither was smiling. Baker had a bit of a smirk—a highly satisfied look, an ugly look.

—What's happened is a briefing went down tonight with liaison from the Bosniaks. They are pissed exceedingly. Reference the spy observed getting a tour of their lines by us. Emphasis not my own. The word used is es pee why.

—Way wait, Henry said. Let me grab my notebook here.

—You don't need any notebook, Baker said.

—This's not a story, Lacroix said.

Baker looked at Lacroix. —Just real life.

Lacroix ignored Baker. Henry decided he didn't like the fixed way Lacroix kept staring at him now.

—Guys, he said.

Lacroix said: —Do you understand? The Bosniaks have their balls in tiny knots on this. By no means can this be described as minor, Henry. The statement of fact, according to them, is we have given a Serbian a tour of their lines down here. There will be no cooperation until this question is settled. None. Henry.

—So there is a story, Henry said, speaking thickly.

They watched him, these invaders of his sleep.

—You've woken me up here guys, Jesus.

Baker continued to sneer. —Henry.

—What?

—Henry. Mate. Thinking-cap time eh.

—What? What?

—Henry, Lacroix said. Henry. You are the spy.

All of a sudden Henry could read the ugly satisfaction in Baker's face for what it was: pure essence of schadenfreude. His mouth grew slowly dry. He felt his heart shift in his chest and became awake and utterly concentrated in his present.

—Fuck off, he said.

—First, Lacroix said, give me your passport.

—Fuck off.

—I'm serious okay Henry.

—My passport.

—A step at a time mate, Baker said. Step at a time.

—We'll send your passport to firstly prove, A, you're not even Serbian.

—Which you're not, right? Ha ha.

—No, Henry said.

Lacroix said: —Passport shows place of birth. We'll need your press card too of course. They'll do their own checking with the UN.

—I'm a reporter.

—Henry, Baker said. These are The Haji's boys. You're seen today on the Bison, taking shots. Someone said the word Serb.

—What. I look like a Serb. What.

Baker cocked his head, smirking. —Little bit, yes, rather. Got that thin face, the black hair. What is your background anyway?

—What?

—Graham, Lacroix said to Baker, with a look.

—Just asking.

Henry stroked his face, hot and tight and aglow, and now also deeply untrustworthy in this strange and restricted world, somehow a sender of cryptic accusations. The nape of his neck was trembling slightly. He suffered a mental flash of himself crucified in the black ring of a telescopic sight, riding high and grinning and waving like a village idiot and Pigeon saying how the captains would never be the ones to have to clean up the brains blown out across the green steel.

—Well. Rotten genetic luck in the circumstances, Baker said. Regardless.

—We'll all just go over in the morning first thing, Lacroix said.

—I beg your pardon, Henry said. We will do no such.

—Listen to us please Henry, Baker said. Do yourself the favor.

—Step two I'm saying, Lacroix said.

—Listen you shitkickers, Henry said. I'm not any Serb. I'm a Canadian citizen. A journalist.

Baker had his palms up. —Do not panic. All right? Do not panic on us Henry. We take these situations step by step as they happen.

—Don't fucking patronize me.

—Hey.

—You limey shit. Don't.

—Henry, relax, Lacroix said.

—I'm not going over anywhere. And no one's taking my passport away from me.

Baker glanced at Lacroix. Lacroix said: —Calm down now. You're making this out of proportion.

Baker picked up the cup and smiled. —Here, have some java Henry. All this is, the Bosniaks want to debrief you.

Henry reached for the cup. Halfway there he saw his hand was trembling and took it back, annoyed with its betrayal.

—We go over to the police station, Lacroix was saying, just here in Ključ, all of us, together. We'll wait right there for you. A brief investigation, I don't know, an hour, two? Some questions. They'll see you are no spy, obviously, wrap it up, you come out, file closed. We're laughing.

—Oh sure, Henry said.

Their faces seemed very close and unnecessarily grave. They had been talking overdeliberately and too loudly to him, Henry noticed, as if he were a mental patient or a lost child or an exhausted recruit drowning in the dust and pain of boot camp. This understanding added smolder to his resentment. He felt like stomping Baker's smirk.

—Look. I don't know these people. Maybe they decide to keep me. What you ganna do then.

—Now why would they do that? Lacroix said.

—So you go then. I'll sign a proxy.

—Ha ha, Baker said.

—Really, Lacroix said. The chances are nothing.

—Nothing.

—Well.

—Nothing. Zero.

—Well. Like nothing, Lacroix said.

—Virtually, Baker said.

Henry had his palms up. —Oh be fucking straight with me guys.

Lacroix said: —In theory...

Henry's hands sank and he swayed back with his mouth turned down at the edges. Baker lowered his eyes to the concrete, as if ashamed to be a witness. He cleared his throat after a bit, said: —Unfortunately there is no other way. To us it may be a joke but to them it is bloody serious as cancer, and they're the ones that count in this sector.

—You have to go, Lacroix said. For everyone's sake. General Rose on down. I'm serious.

—Hell I do, Henry said.

—You do. You really do.

—Well I disagree, compadre. And I'm a free citizen of Canada and a neutral journalist.

—No one's saying you're not, Lacroix said. But let's keep a perspective please. All they want is to verify you're no Chetnik. The procedure is minor.

—Fine. Fax them my credentials. Let them verify.

—Here's the thing, Baker said. They say they know you are a Serb spy because this spy on the back of our Bison taking photographs resembling a Serb, he also happened to be flashing Serb victory signs all up and down the valley.

—Serb signs, Henry said.

Both captains snorted. Baker said: —Victory signs. Never

underestimate the brute power of paranoia in a war zone. A spy flashing the Serb salute. Look at me look at me.

More snorting.

Lacroix said: —We told him of course you wouldn't know a Serb sign if it chewed your ass cheeks off. That you're just off the Herc in Zagreb this morning. No, he says. Uh uh. He is adamant, this officer. This guy of yours is a spy, this guy was signaling Greater Serbia Forever or whatever the three fingers are supposed to mean.

Henry's gaze had set on Lacroix's right hand: three pronged digits, two tucked to the palm. Gooseskin clawed the flesh of Henry's back, his belly fluxed and a pulse of blood moved in a dark wash through his paining head.

—People saw him, Lacroix was saying. All day long there are multiple witnesses and—get this—there are also pictures. We said okay show us. He said they will, tomorrow.

This detailing of how patent the ridiculousness of the affair had raised new merriness in both captains, who now converted their snorting to outright laughter. The old ease was back of a sudden. All was well.

—There should be a name for this, Baker said. Some syndrome. Postwar espionage hallucination.

—But doesn't matter what they think, Lacroix said. It's only hard evidence that carries a damn, and that in truth there's nothing of. We'll go in and you'll talk honestly. You've done nothing wrong. We'll go over in the morning and settle it. This's why step one is let's get our evidence organized—the documents first, the passport and the press card. All right Henry? Let's focus on that for right now.

Henry sat very still.

—Spy boy, Baker said. He leaned over and clapped Henry's shoulder. Chin up, double oh seven.

—Okay? Lacroix said.

—Okay, Henry told them. His voice faraway and tiny.

Henry was moving in the still night, beneath the massed stars. To his right stood the perimeter fence. The Bisons were parked in a line out to his left. The ex-factory behind him now. He had a pack with a red maple leaf, two foot long, sewn across its flap and a stuffed sleeping bag lashed above. His camera bag was strapped to the underside. He had little idea of what he was doing. He kept walking. Once or twice he tripped in the scrub. Presently he had outrun the Bisons. He touched the light on his wristwatch—three twelve in the a.m., partner. He steadied himself. Easy now. Then he bent over and retched up dark bile and elongating stalactites of acidic mucus.

He wiped his mouth backhandedly and went on. His eyes adjusted fully and he didn't stumble anymore. When he looked back the sodium lights at the factory were small as landlocked stars. The perimeter was a chain-link fence with razor rolls on the ground before it and taut wires for the trip flares, and sandbags also, sandbags aplenty. It was mostly unlit. He took off his pack and sat on it and held his head. After a while he chewed three aspirin. The man with the radioactive face, he thought. Nothing to do but cry. He didn't cry. He shivered grossly and considered his foul luck. He settled himself. The thing to do was to make his way to Sarajevo. Find the consulate. Get them to get his passport back from the officers. He rose calmly and stooped for his pack. The thing to do was to find a means of crossing the perimeter or exiting the guarded main gate. Some bluff or artifice. Some form of resolution and resourcefulness. It would have to be done.

He heard a click a few feet off to his left and his head shot up. He was perfectly still. Another click sounded dead ahead, at a farther distance. Then another, in time, to the right. He strained his eyes till they ached. When another came he thought: Stone, as he sensed a larger shifting in behind, in the texture of the blackness, something serpentine, monstrous, and then it came fast and he let out dog noises, his body convulsing electrically, limbs stickstiff. He rolled, was right over.

—Hooboo, a voice spoke.

Henry merely lay and was rigid but for the heart, the crazed heart, thrashing like an independent animal fighting to tear out and away from him, the doomed body. A man was against the galaxy with hands akimbo. —Hooboo, the form spoke again. Hooboo. Ah Jesus that is great. Then folded over its own laughter, low and guttural.

Henry began to stammer.

—Humma humma humma, the form said, straightening. Now it's hum fuckun humma. Even better. You're a living classic, guy.

The form came forward and sank and the starshine lit onto a bubble face with a meandering hairline.

—Pigeon.

Henry sat himself slowly up. He had never known that mental shock could sock you from the inside like a physical blow—not to this extent: your own blood turned to spikes.

—Pigeon, he said again.

—Humma humma, Corporal Pigeon told him, chuckling. Here. I'll butt you.

—No, Henry said.

—Take it.

—Don't. Smoke.

—For nerves and whatnot.

—You, Henry said.

Pigeon smiled and his teeth weren't beige but starlit. He withdrew the pack and plucked one and lit it for himself. —Funny what you meet on these midnight rambles. Taking a constitutional under the stars. How you is guy?

The words spoken in that methodical inching pace, while Henry couldn't seem to find his breath at all.

—It's this point of interest, Pigeon said. Two of us a-meeting. Point of coincidence.

—You're a funny man, Henry said. Everyone loves a prankster.

—No sir, Pigeon said.

—Don't quite know if you understand, Henry said.

—The rich deep shit I have sunk you in? And he laughed gutturally.

—It's not a joke, Henry said. He shook his fists with thumbs and two neighboring fingers jutting. His friendly greeting to the people of the Bihac. —Har fucking har, he said. Burn the new asshole. The hilarity. You know what you've gone and caused me? You even comprehend?

Pigeon took a new drag with his right hand, the point of his smoke welling orange as his left hand rose with a matching Serbian salute then slowly turned around; he clenched in the thumb and first finger, leaving just one, the middle, rigid. —Well there she is reporter boy what I think of what I caused. Sit smart and swivel nicely. You and all your journalism fraternity. How much I give an unruly fuck.

Henry didn't say anything. Became aware instead of the logistics of his predicament. Factors sank in. Truly how it was that this corporal happened to be out here so close to the dawn. In the silence Henry looked to the far lights again, and back.

—Gone shy all a sudden, reporter man.

Henry held the fingers of one hand in those of the other, bent them till some knuckles softly cracked. —You following me. Watching me?

—Woo—but your arse be frying in the battery acid tonight, my son.

—Not a joke, Henry muttered, looking over his shoulder.

—No sirree.

—Pigeon, how d'you know what my situation is, one way or another.

—The people here have this tradition. If you bring some good news they have to give you a gift. What's your gift?

—What's your news?

Pigeon coughed and when he went on his voice had changed by some namelessly subtle yet unmistakably profound degree. He began to describe a village high up through the woods that his patrol had come upon the previous fall. A basement full of children and that the place had been set to flame with paint thinner under a high sky all blue like crystal you could have sworn to have reached to and touched. And how they burned his gloves to the hands, these kids, all like charcoal, come apart and crumbled through his very fingers.

—That's news. There's your news, boy.

And how the old man of the village had been splayed in the square and someone—*they*—had carved off his hams and made him eat his own dying flesh still hot with his own blood, and it was in his mouth and blood in his bulging open eyes, his beard as red as satanskin and bolts through every joint of every limb to a pine table underneath. How they'd made a little fire of his privates. Sliced off his eyelids so he couldn't stop seeing and move back into himself, all through his own slow dying. How they'd used a barn to pen the womenfolk. Women who looked to be ninety years old some, and little girls others, no difference. Certain things done to them with animals and there were milk cows and rams and throats slashed open and blood to the ankles sloshing in there, all the white skin of the women all spattered. Some were found in the threshing machine that had jammed on so many of their long bones and the fatty baffling of their soft thighs. Axes and sledgehammers mostly were what had finished them. How the smell from up off the blood was like a gas that made a person vomit it was that thick. How they went on and in the woods the men were all tied with elbows pulled together behind them and their noses and lips cut off, eyes dug out, some with spoons and sometimes the spoons that had done the digging still laying on the ground with the jellied eyeball in or next to. Some with their pants down and testicles nailed through to the trunks or the roots of the trees in the cold earth. And it was reckoned the most were bayoneted or else throatcut as if those who'd done it couldn't stand the waste of a good single bullet and there was a cooking fire making clear they who'd done it were there for a while too, making a festival of it, yeh, Pigeon said, a blood festival. Roasted lamb bones, other bones, piled bottles of slivovitz and vodka and little hills of cigarette butts with stains to show they'd been handled with bloodied fingers. And some of the men were also disemboweled and their wet insides dragged from them and some draped over logs and plainly sodomized after death and some were both so their hanging faces rested on the cold sausage mush of their own intestines. Yeh, Pigeon said. Yeh.

—So we went on through the woods and all the next day and it was pissing a freezing sleet and up past the treeline in the next valley, just mud and rocks, was where we come up on them. The ones responsible.

Henry was watching the earth, feeling his breaths. He didn't want to look at the face close beside him.

—They were a mixed unit, a mongrel unit, Pigeon said, and described:

How they were Croat mostly but also weirdly with Serbs and even could you believe it some Muslims who had done it to their own. Plus the festering scum of a nation apart from the nations of ordinary men altogether, those cut loose from the bowels of jails which split open and spill their polluting foulness into all wars when crime becomes the medium of ordinary life and ordinary goodness a crime in and of itself. These were rapists and molesters of little children, Pigeon said, and murderers of every stripe, thieving cowards and demented backstabbers. Men with weird pinheads and slavering jaws, inbreds and submongrels. Knuckledraggers. But others were only kids of seventeen gone bad in combat, maybe college boys back home. And those who looked all right at first but to look in their eyes was to see the eyes of wolves not men. And older men with slack wrinkled faces such like Pigeon said he'd never seen before at all or even believed plausible.

—We caught them up all right but we had white armor and blue helmets then and nothing but observer status and hell if everyone didn't know what toothless dogs it was that we were.

He narrated to Henry how quite a few of them could even speak English but what they could do and what actually came out of their crazed mouths was a whole different effing ball game. That they had tied clothes on their heads, wore earrings and various pieces of women's jewelery. Colordyed pieces of different uniforms and spike helmets from the Great War and swastika ones from the last and one had on a brassiere and one a woman's long blond wig crusty stained with dark blood dried and another had makeup like a streetcorner whore and another with a fake wood leg on the back of his belt like a tail and one in all that chill was naked but for boots and he remembered had painted a skull on his torso in some other's blood human or animal who knew. And one was wearing chains on which were hung every kind of implement and item you could imagine so that it all jangled like a suit of loose armor such like Pigeon had never believed he'd see outside of a fever. Saws and kettles and bottles and pliers and hammers and potlids and handguns. And one showed Pigeon a bag he had full of noses. They were all of them drunk and stoned and whatever they said was gibberish and they couldn't stop talking.

—But it weren't any chemical what was in them that made them so high.

Henry coughed. —An awful lot you seem to know.

Not so much even the taste of blood, Pigeon doggedly explained, rather what it was he'd seen right off was how in those mountains up there in the cold remove the pack of boys and men together had transmogrified themselves and become gods, actual not movie gods, gods like the ones in old Greece on a mountain that stood not far at all from that very place.

—Gods, he said. You understand me? What I'm talking.

—Pigeon, Henry said. Listen.

—When I say gods man I mean not some feeling inside. But when you know as sure as you have a right arm that anything you choose to do is yours to do—everything.

—Gods. Right. Yes.

—Yes. They were just a pretty little party of god monsters up above the treeline, prowling round. Like that first man before the one true God introduced himself. And I'll tell you the best part, guy. The real news.

—I don't think I want to know, Henry said. His voice had gone soft.

—The villages were in a safe zone. Yeh. A guaranteed safe zone by the governments of all the world.

—Yes, Henry said, nodding and sincere now. Tragic.

—Say which?

—Tragic.

—Tragic?

—Yes. Absolutely.

—And why is it you say that, press.

—Pardon me?

—You heard.

—Because it is. Like you said.

—When'd I say anything about any tragedy?

—…

—Well is it or isn't it. Henry.

—Look, Pigeon.

—I asked a straight question.

—It is. It's a tragedy, of course.

—Bull. Sheet.

Henry sniffed carefully.

—You think I felt sorry for them Muslims? The burn kids and the bolted old man.

—Pigeon, I don't know what you felt.

—Damn right you don't. But I will tell you. I looked at em and I thought, Pathetic. To let someone do that to you. You think you deserve the right to honor? Fuck that. Honor is dying well. That's all that is. One death to each, that there it is, the ball game.

—What did you do?

—What did we do. Used the radio to report. We took the mute girl off them, s'all.

—The who?

—They'd kept one Muslim girl for a takeaway. Blond. They all kept talking gibberish. What you do takes hold of the mind. Gibberish pissing from the mouths a hundred miles an hour. Animal noises. Their eyes like glass or wolves. I'm telling you they were turned into gods and their bodies didn't know to handle the change. We walked the mute girl out of there. They went over the hill and that was the last of our zone. If no one fires on you you do nothing but report in.

He lowered the cigarette and quashed its spark on his sole and stripped the butt to fibers he let go but the still air did nothing to bear these scraps away.

—Going back now, Henry said. I have to try and sleep.

—Uh huh.

—They're taking me in the police station in the morning.

—That they are. Get you alone in that room they have.

Henry listened to his own breathing and spoke not.

—Question is, what a they decide on doing to you in this

particular room. Got you alone. Who can know.

Henry heaved himself up on butterfly legs. Felt leaden and cold but for his tight shining face, shivered. He'd inverted himself in, the heat all wired wrong, his core exposed.

—I'll show you a thing.

—I'm going.

He stooped for his bag. Pigeon reached around. Then he was holding out an unsheathed bayonet.

Some time passed. —Okay, Henry said.

—What's your hurry partner?

—Sleep, Henry said. I should.

—Siddown, Pigeon said.

—Thanks, no.

—The journalism fraternity. The high and the mighty gentle-folk of the press. Fly in and see. Spread the word of truth. The drunk who killed the two but you couldn't say, was that truth Henry? Explain it to me. Tell me why is it the black birds come to swingtown.

—I think I.

—Sit.

—I.

—Sit.

Henry didn't sit exactly. He kept his eyes on the blade and settled into half of a squat. Started to edge the pack around between them.

—Because you said to me you wanted to put only the truth down.

—Yes.

—The truth which is your job.

—Yes.

—You fuckun liar. You're all sick dogs and you pant for it.

Henry waited. Pigeon held the bayonet angled to the starlight. Both sides appeared razorhoned.

—I seen it also when you had that C8 to play with. In the eyes.

—You pushed it on me.

—Yeh it's me. Henry how you going to talk truth if you don't walk with it first.

—What is this Pigeon.

Pigeon covered his odd hairline with one palm and became almost kindly. —My friend, it's because I care. That I look out for you.

Henry grimaced. —I am sorry if I don't understand what you're saying. But this is not sense to me. I'm going now. I'm going Pigeon. His legs had begun to cramp. He put them into gear and made them expand beneath him, rising. A very tough slow six inches then it was twelve then he was almost up.

—Hey hey, Pigeon said, lackadaisically.

—Keep going, Henry said, a thought spilling out as sound. He lifted his pack and backed away then turned and, to his surprise, was making paces and beginning to feel calm. All right. Only his nape goosepimpled. And then *thud thud thud* from behind and he began to spring into a run and the pack was wrenched, the strap yanking his looped shoulder back and around. He sat down hard.

—The fuck you think you are, press, Pigeon said. Ungrateful. You asshole.

Henry heard a note of hysterical whining somewhere in his own respirations. Pigeon tapped the top of his head with the flat of the bayonet. —I'm the only one, my son. I've got the true news, no one else even cares.

—The only one, Henry said.

—Yes.

—The only one what?

Pigeon sank. —My son, he said. My son, you see anyone else out here, looking to help?

—Look, please.

—You're going in a room with The Haji's boys. Big Mr. I., hisself.

—I'm asking, Henry said.

—They're going to let them eat you eh. Alive.

—Pigeon, listen.

—Man I'm the only one.

—But this is because of you.

—What?

—I'm sorry. They've got my passport.

—There's the real you, Pigeon said. Do you suppose?

—I don't…

—That's why they are going to nail you, dipshit. You know it's true and I know it and that's what you are, a spy. Dirty spy bastard.

—Please, Henry said. Pigeon Jesus just please let me go.

—Spy.

—Okay, Henry said. Okay now. The knife tapped his head again.

—Up spy, up.

As in a thousand Westerns, Henry had bunched a load of grit in his right fist. Now all he had to do was rise and wheel and fling it into the face of his enemy. Well here he was. He looked up and saw the razor steel, starlit and closeby, and then the inkcones of the eyes above, backed into the bubble face. As easy as running the vertical marble face of a cliff in bowling shoes. He opened the ridiculous fist and, with a hoist from Pigeon's free hand, came to his feet. Swayed. His guts were water.

—I'm just helping you my son, Pigeon said. I'm the only one. He delivered a compact shove to Henry and they started moving away from the perimeter and the lights both. Let's get out the truth, he said. There can be no bullshit here between us.

There was nothing Henry could do to quell a steep whine rising in his throat with each breath.

—Yeh you're a spy, Pigeon murmured.

—What does that even mean?

—Spy.

—Okay spy.

—Admit.

Henry fell quiet, trying to decide whether talking or silence would best do. His hot face throbbed. After a time he said: —Explain how I could be a Serb spy. All the way from Montreal.

No answer.

—Let's stop and think a second, Pigeon.

—Is it thinking or is it knowing.

Henry decided the silence option was the prudent course at this juncture. Pigeon started singing, softly. They came to a ditch which could not have been natural. It was too steep and deep and stretched away on both sides, curved off. Maybe for drainage.

—Now get down in there, Pigeon said. Henry hesitated and Pigeon stabbed the air before his face with the brilliant steel. Henry gasped and stumbled back. Pigeon gave him a tender kick and he slithered down the bank. Pigeon jumped after.

—Wait there, he said, producing a flashlight. Down here they can't spot a light. Safe if you aim low.

Henry sunk down, listened to his drumming pulses, observed the stars in their gawking masses above the walls around him. The flashlight scratched at his eyes. —Up.

Henry stood and blinked.

—Go.

Henry lifted the pack. They walked for a bit. —Here, Pigeon said. Lookit. Here. The beam dropped on a rock.

—Move that. Henry went forward and moved the rock; there was a hollow behind it. In the hollow was a steel pot.

—Go on. Lift the lid.

Henry knelt and did as directed. There was a ball of aluminum foil.

—Give it.

An organic hothouse reek tinged with the dull carbon whiff of something charred and chemical emanated from the ball as he passed it across. Then he held the light as directed. Pigeon unwrapped the foil bundle and thereby exposed a blackened tube and a sticky chunk of brownsugarish substance underneath a blooming whiff so rich and fruited it spiked the barrels of both Henry's nostrils and made his eyes narrow.

—A fat weight of gooey time, my man, Pigeon was murmuring. Lookit. Time itself. Time as a solid.

Quickly he prepared the substance on a section of foil and lit a candle nub brought up from the selfsame pot and set the foil with its balanced cargo over the flame, the nub wedged tight in the soil beneath. He had driven the dagger into the earth similarwise at his right heel and motioned Henry to approach now with a crooked fanning of his freed fingers.

—I prefer not.

—Comes a time in every life to man up and chase down a little dragon.

—I prefer not.

—Henry, the zone of preference has been left far far behind.

He gave Henry the tube and Henry held it quaveringly as Pigeon held the flame and bade him puff while the viscous drop like a mercury demon with a tiny evaluating mind of its own veered scuttling from the point of the tube, seeking cringing refuge in the foil wrinkles.

—Hunt it out. Fill up your beefy lungs, son. Breathe down the dragon's tail and breathe it not out.

Henry coughed. He saw one hand leave the foil and enfold in its core the dagger hilt. —I said draw, Henry. Draw deep.

—Okay. All right.

When he was done he sat back in a vortex of numb planetary spinning and it was Pigeon's turn. Quick puffs were executed and Pigeon sighed. A vertigo had meanwhile gathered its center at the base of Henry's skull and grounded there raised the hood of his self and hurled him out forward into eternal massed whirling blackness. —Something's wrong.

—Go with it.

—Something's wrong. I'm going to die.

An unpalatable heat leeched to his skin. He felt tattered and softened in his own frame. Felt the ropes of sickly nausea down his gut tauten upward under the heeling glory madness of his blacked-out vision and queered tumbling mind. —I shouldn't have. I shouldn't have. Oh God fuck me I should never have.

He had his palms flat on either side of him as if they were stabilizers but the planet would not stabilize. Howling gravities tore at his flanks. When he could, when his cosmic descent had slowed, he opened his eyes and saw Pigeon readying a third trap for the holy condiment, the drop of distilled resin like the essence of a fallen star, blessed sap of the Hindu Kush. He smoked of it and presented the remainder to Henry, who flinched.

—Take yourself in hand.

—No. No more.

—There isn't any no here, Henry. Take.

—What in God's sheer name I ever do to you dude? What.

Henry sat up and puffed at this humid taste and his tissues convulsed at once. He rolled away like a hurt dog and vomit burst past his teeth. He hunched on all fours like a dog not hurt this time but one with a bitch in heat at its belly and he heaved and humped and though he had retched only mucus before now the convulsions reached so deep they dredged up the food of the day. The mess chow and strong army coffee. Flecks of aspirin. All.

—Virgin, Pigeon said. He used the flashlight to find the fallen works and then set a fourth load for his lungs and brain to consume in the same manner that plants ate of sunlight through a mystery osmosis of ether to cell, the ethereal given up to the solid, the pure to the complex and diaphanous to earthen, that which endures to that which passes every instant backward into the nothings and nothingness of spent time.

He heard Pigeon asking if he'd ever seen the end of time.

—I have. Not.

The vertigo was like seeing the stars and the sand and the night as radically demarcated images like photos in a strip of film looped and jerkily running through the projector of his brow.

—There is a great message at the end of time. It's a triumph. See it. The time in which each object will be given the power of voice so that they might call out if an infidel should cower there behind them. Then they will all be slain.

—Slain. What.

—Slain. There is a mighty purity to the end of time, Henry. It took The Haji to show to me this truest of light.

—Imamovic. You know Imamovic.

—Do you know where I'm from Henry?

Henry held his face, his radioactive face. The world had calmed; it was falling away sleepily then rising again, like a wave, everything soft and softened. A glow of pleasure was building in his tissues so sweet it made his teeth sing.

—There's a river fat and black that cuts English from French through Indian land. The last red wolves in the last mixed forests. The lumbermills and the logjams. Fiddlers. The whitewater chutes, the falls and covered bridges. Hockey rinks and parliament.

—The Ottawa valley, you're talking.

—The black forests. Only a quarter of me is an Algonquin clan but that's enough. Blood don't dissolve like salt in a tincture. Nor bone.

—O fuck I'm so fucked I'm so so fucked, Henry said. Heat in his gut instead of nausea now, fingers of flame stabbing the bone hoops of his rib cage. But the building pleasure was so dense now he wanted to somehow eat it, his mouth stuffed with the sweet nougat of its fluxing, eat it down and swallow this endless pleaser.

—You'll be a-okay.

—How—how'd you know him?

—After that day up in the mountains under the crystal sky, that village, I felt a change in me. I took myself ay wol. Took a pack and put in it a round of cheese, rye bread, a jug of water. Hiked off. I was five days in the mountains on my own, trying to avoid the different lines all through the forests, the trenches and the snipers. But I knew it couldn't last. Day six I was taken. They brought me to Imamovic. He was in a cave and surrounded by Arabs. His face had a light. Not the dead light like in the eyes of those pagan savages who blew through that Muslim village, not a light gone bad but the opposite, a thing pure and of peace.

Imamovic. He has a beard and he dresses in white. He asked me who I was and I told the truth. He touched my shoulders and looked me in the face and I felt something new in me, I swear.

A muttering undertone held a counterpoint to these words that fascinated Henry until he slowly understood it was his own mouth working.

—They brought a translator, Pigeon was saying, and then The Haji asked me about who I was when I was small and I told him that too the truth. And he said that he was like me. Then he said words that stamped right straight in my memory forever.

Pigeon pressed at his head, concentrating. His voice came out strained and higher, pinched down, with a nasal near melody to its new rhythm almost like a chant. He recounted how The Haji spoke. How he said he had always been like a sapling cut of its root and replanted but that such a replanting could never support the great tree that real men are supposed to become. Said, the soul of the root was only nourished by one kind of soil and his people, the Bosniak, had long ago lost this good and true anchor. Said, the men who were with him there were true desert sons and had come to revive his people not merely with arms but with the indestructible strength of the true faith, the eternal truth, hard and pure as the desert from which they'd come, the desert now set to inundate and overrun the soft green breast of this Europe, this forested illusion that had drained the old faith and caused its rot. Said, what had made them weak so that they were now become as rabbits under the falcon's wings and talons of the infidel was the slow diminution of the old ways over centuries. Said how in this green soil the ceremonies had dwindled and the fire in the first words was allowed to become just warmth. Said, but now the men from the desert had entered Europe through gashes torn by the atrocities inflicted by the infidels on the believers and that this had been the hidden destiny of this diminished corner of the true faith all along, dictated by the secret workings of the Most Merciful, to languish till this very moment in which to readmit the sons of the desert to burst into Europe's hearth where the churches once stood but had now rotted out from within and were ready to collapse like a barn infested by woodworm for too long. A new century coming. Said, nothing in the whole world would now ever be the same.

Henry was meanwhile seeing odd shapes butted against his vision and his mood was more subtle in the cradle of its pleasuring, demi-hidden forms kept both nimbly ahead of his self yet also trod with an air of piperish exultance, shining him on. He did not whoop. He came back to Pigeon's words as Pigeon was saying: —...I saw we were the same. He and I, me and my Native blood. That we both lost our ancient self by tryna merge with white men ways, instead of keeping apart and pure. Ancients' ways that never can die.

—They pay him you know. Imamovic. Pay him rent here.

—They don't understand. No one has words. I seen the heroes. Pure as the desert, ready to die. None like them have been before in the world, like what is happening here and flowing from it. Like what is coming. I have seen the end of time. When the sky brings flames. When those who hide behind stones get called out by the stones for the pure ones to come slaughter.

—Pigeon.

—Get up. Get up, Weintraub.

Henry thought about this, using his muzzled mind as best he could to fumble at the strangeness in the phrase and try to trace its cause. —You know my name.

—I know what it means. I know what you are, press.

—Pigeon. What is this.

—They changed me up there. They washed my soul. I touched my forehead to a rug. I saw the truest light there is. They taught me who are the devils and what his faces are, how he whispers. I know you Henry J. Weintraub, birthplace Montreal, Quebec.

Pigeon fiddled at the top pocket of his cargo pants, produced something, flicked it. It slapped Henry's chest. He looked down at his lap and saw a crowned coat of arms. —How? he said.

—There are no limits no more. Not for me.

Henry opened the passport in the dark and starshine came off the silvered outline of his own photograph.

—The devil has a curved nose, Weintraub. They taught me. Oh my stars they taught me and they opened my eyes.

Henry licked drily at his own lips. He looked to his pack and assembled himself, through the mist of the sap in his blood. —How'd you get this Pigeon?

—But I have to help. To show to you a merciful favor, my friend.

—Yes.

—Get you out. He checked his watch. Henry took the

moment to shove the passport in his pocket and get his feet under him, his hands to the pack. No, he thought, leave it. His hands moved so slowly.

—The eternal wanderer, Pigeon said. Sit your ass.

—No, Henry said.

Pigeon got up and gestured with the blade. Henry got up, shouldering his pack.

—Don't look a gift horse. Where else you got to go?

Henry considered this.

—Going to get you out, chump, Pigeon said.

—Why?

—I want to.

—But I'm the devil.

—Yes but you said you want to tell the truth. But you got to live the truth to tell it. And I'm going to get you out.

—How?

—This way. There.

Henry moved where he must. They trod the path inside the trench walls in silence and the axis of the planet tilted under Henry's swaying. The heat was suffused in his skin and the drug moved its sickly glimmering sap through the honeycombed machine works of his brain. Heady ferment of some Afghan's fruited poppy bulb, all the flinted desert's span in that brewed milky ooze, saltzinc and sulphur, the green movement of the vegetable blood, a balm most tender for the mind's distress.

Where the track terminated they waited. Wire was visible at the breaking soil above. Pigeon kept consulting his watch. Then he held the wires high for Henry to shove his pack through and then climb after. Henry found himself on a splitfaced slope, just beyond the wire. Gradually he noticed there were upright shapes in the moonwash with insectile prongs, like the confirming symptoms of a dread and dreadedly suspected disease. Henry looked at them and thought woozily how this is it, here is the nexus of all your life's trajectories. All the breaths and all the touches, the tiny frozen moments when you stared through windows or picked at the tip of your nose. The gestures you made at breakfast from habit, your fingers on all those keyboards making symbols in rows. Each one of these out of a life like cells in the body of this one living moment.

He decided calmly he was not going to go out into that minefield with a maniac at his back. There was a physical logic that flowed from this decision. He shook his slackened limbs.

When he turned Pigeon was climbing up under the wire. There was a moment to strike which Henry watched pass. Pigeon got up. He had put off the flashlight and slipped it loosely into a pocket of his cargo pants and now took a long tube from another which he held horizontally, his other hand around the knife handle whose blade goaded Henry forward. This new horizontal light clicked on and threw out a bar of purple aluminum shine—a blacklight that lit up glowing marks on the rocks in amongst the mines that some contriving hand had etched in paint of a sort ordinarily invisible.

Henry picked up the pack and, shouldering one strap, moved off gingerly. The visible pronged mines were like a pineapple crop around them on the slope. The buried ones had their nonvisual presences in his thoughts.

—So long as you follow those signs, Pigeon said. Just so long.

Henry started to speak.

—Better if you're quiet, Pigeon said. Better all round. Then:
—Just you catch those signs.

Henry threaded his way carefully down the slope. There was scree and rock, some tough bushes. As they descended he began to see the road which curved off about the rise to the left, a paler swoosh like a wide stroke laid in salt over the night plain. He could hear the river and Pigeon looked back to make sure they were below the sightlines of the wires to their rear then drew the flashlight and pointed it ahead, pulsing the light thrice. A moment after, four sharp pulses came back from across the far side of the road and then an engine, probably a motorcycle's, kicked over and softly panted.

—Go ahead now.

—Pigeon.

—Hush it.

—Who is that?

—When you have a pure heart, Pigeon said, a heart white and pure and cold like a diamond.

—Pigeon. What is this?

—Devil, speak not.

And they reached a level ridge overlooking the road and running toward it, apparently free of mines, unlike the slopes falling off on either side. Walking out along it, Henry began to think as he'd never in his life: calculus like a throb in the temples.

—If I'm going missing then what.

—Missing, Pigeon said.

—They think I ran.

—Which you did.

—You set this up. You set it from the beginning.

—You want to tell the truth don't you. You'll have a message to tell, press. Oh yes. Tell to the whole world.

Henry turned and they faced each other.

—Get going. There's nowheres else. Go.

Henry glanced at the flashlight loose in the cargo pocket and inhaled. Pigeon waggled the blade. —What?

—You going to cut me.

—Not if I don't have to.

—Of course. He slid his hand under the pack strap on his shoulder as he turned away then turned sharply back, jerking the strap off, driving the pack with his forearm into Pigeon. His other hand dipped low, going for the flashlight. Pigeon teetered on the lip of the ridge, his knife hand flailing behind him for balance. The pack had dropped and Henry slid on one knee, his fingers only just brushing the flashlight loose. Pigeon made one scratching grab with his left hand as he went over, his nails tearing lines across Henry's brow.

Henry picked up the flashlight and put it on as Pigeon scrambled back up. He laid the beam on the bubble face, filling Pigeon's eyes with shine, then stood on the blade. Pigeon muttered and clawed at the light and fell on his chest. He let go the knife and Henry bent for it. Pigeon reared, the crown of his hard head taking Henry unexpectedly in under the shortribs, a pylon shock that popped the wind from him and made him drop the light and sat him down hard over the far side of the ridge.

He started to slide down and scrambled madly.

Pigeon huffed. —You want some.

Henry had thrashed up back onto the ridge. He lunged and got handfuls of the man's shirt and kept heaving. His one thought was to keep him from the fallen blade, the breaths acid and ragged through his teeth. Pigeon swore and his shirt broke. He shoved and bent forward, maybe to find the knife. Henry jacked his knee up hard and got back the token of a satisfying crunch, a grunt. Then there was a black space and he was down on his belly and tasting blood and hearing a shrilled tone like an alarmed cat constant in one ear.

He felt a feather stroke of passing air over his face as he rolled to a knee and Pigeon hopped and when another kick came Henry held his arms crossed before his face like a bone crucifix. The *thwock* of leather contact from the slogging boot rode its shock broadly through his torso and sat him flat again with clicking teeth. He kicked up and felt a heel contact. Then he saw the flashlight, and scratched for it.

—Fucker, Pigeon was saying. Devil filth.

The boots he took didn't hurt; nothing hurt much; it was the holy narcotic cotton stuffing his nerves.

Henry rolled over with the flashlight and swept the beam and found the bubble face, made it blink. There was blood on the teeth. —Jew, it spat.

Henry got his feet under him and jumped to the left, keeping the beam aimed. Pigeon struck the air two-fistedly to the right, like a man trying to beat out flames. Henry lashed in with his free hand—contact was a rubbery sensation, smacking the open meat plate of another man's face at full bare swing.

Pigeon pivoted with a fluidity almost graceful and this time Henry saw the blow that made his jaw explode. A great weariness passed down one numb side. The beam drooped. Concentrate, he thought. There were hosts of buzzing things about him, tiny and twirling.

He ducked his chin but Pigeon's foot like a brick took him in the fork of his thighs. He didn't feel the magnitude of the damage for a moment, as he was lifted, then twin suns of acid rose up from the pits of his balls and he wanted to cry with the sting of it, opiated or not, as Pigeon drove him back off the ridge, kneeling on his chest as they slid a little way down the loose slope. Pigeon grabbed his ears and banged his skull to the sand. He crossed his forearms, sinking his hands inside Henry's collars and twisting and pulling, bearing down hard with a Judo choke that crimped flat the soft tissue of Henry's windpipe, made blood vault in his spiraling brain and his face fatten with the pressure of the hold. He did nothing and his eyes were bulbous in their sockets over the blooming lips. Seams of blackness split his view and a dead metal buzz rose in both ears.

He hit up weakly at the crossed arms but they were cinched in like bolted steel. Another ache from his wounded balls throbbed in his deep belly. This was the finale, nullity. When a creature no longer can or wants to defend itself the world moves in. All things are doomed and all things devour and are devoured. From Henry's right hand slowly filtered the information that the flashlight was still there. Skinned down to one last receding essence, he lifted and chopped upward, aiming with the base, going for the eyes. There was some very solid jarring, some brittle crackling, and the pressure eased. Pigeon caught the flashlight and twisted it loose, rolling off Henry in the process. Henry drew in a shuddering load of night air and was feasted at his core on the multiplicative gifts of oxygen. Life and power.

Pigeon slithered back up to the ridge. Henry followed, full of terror for the mines around and below. He slumped over the crest close to where Pigeon panted. —It's okay, he said. Henry saw he had his palm pressed to the side of his face. He expected Pigeon would try to find the knife now but he did not, he only sat up a bit: —Anything left press?

—Leave me.

Pigeon snorted; a liquid gurgle in a busted nose. A long stretch of empty hurting time passed.

—Passport, Henry said. How'd you.

—Commander's office.

Henry thought for a space. —What the fuck *is* this?

Pigeon looked at his watch, miraculously still on the arm. —Time to. Rock.

—What are they? *What* Pigeon?

—What are they. True servants of fire, my friend. The past and future. Cleansers. They been refined in the desert where it's nothing but death, the purity of death. When I saw these men the first time I knew the truth lives. In them. You know why Weintraub?

—No. I don't. Pigeon.

Another long and ragged pause; maybe Pigeon was gathering himself. Then: —Before they sent me back I watched an attack. Men went down singing and wearing bombs. To wipe themselves and their enemies off the face of this earth. You imagine it Weintraub? I saw purity in their shining faces. They were happy. I never believed a death like that could be. That the will could be there but so peaceful. No one in this world has seen such deaths. But the world's ganna learn. To go to death happy cos you're taking your enemy with you. The faith! Nothing can fight this. The world belongs to these men, Weintraub. They're here now and they never retreat. Do you understand what I am telling you Weintraub?

Henry touched the passport in his pocket to assure himself it was still there then rose. Wearily, Pigeon rose with him. —Where you ganna go? He shook the flashlight. I am your light and your way here, Henry. There's no outs. Henry said all right. Okay. They both swayed close and when Pigeon lowered the beam Henry floppily reared back in one giddy sweeping motion so deep it seemed he would crash over backward but instead he hurled his forehead down and in, maximally, as if his brow were an inanimate thing like the edge of a great ax fullswung, directly into the middle of Pigeon's muttering face. There was an obliterating white crack through his brain.

It was some moments before his self could realign with his body and then Henry realized that his body had not returned to full function but was progressing nonetheless, that it was gibbering like an animal as it fumbled its way downhill.

He stood and looked. He was halfway down the slope, the vile metal prongs everywhere. He breathed. He came to himself as fully as he could. Then he went on downhill through the mines in the dark. He was one fluid will pushing for bottom like a free diver seeking a pearl. He didn't stumble. He moved laterally when he felt the need. He did not question such feelings. He was bent hard over, cringing and rapid. But no flash came, no shock of jagged orange nor spurt of clawing hellfire from below.

He came down through the minefield and when he hit the white gravel of the road he slid on his knees, sobbing, then got up and ran for the water sounds of the river closeby. He lay quiet on the mud in the reedy bank and could smell where they'd burnt garbage in the day. Later he heard the motorcycle accelerate then fade. He listened for hours more but heard no other engines and no footsteps. No one called out. He was dreaming sometimes as he listened and got scared he might be muttering aloud and held his mouth and saw a street and his exwife was there and he tried to talk to her but he was all bound up in a straightjacket. And once he curled up and slept fully for however long and started awake with a kick. He felt for his wristwatch but it was gone. Another time he crawled a distance through the reeds. He got very thirsty and wormed down to the moony water and cupped some of its cold to his mouth and felt how swollen his face was and washed off scabs and dried gobs of blood black as leeches. The moving water sounded to him uncannily like voices when he crawled back in the reeds and lay, imparting to him odd comfort, as if hosts of souls were murmuring in the dark for his benefit alone.

When he at last came back through to the road the sky was starting to pinken. He rose and stood and wiped away the soil and the dirt. All of him hurt now. Parts of his tight face creaked when they shifted. The last of the drug had left him and pain and pain and pain had replaced it. He swallowed it down. He started to march on the dawnlit way and in a while he forgot he was alive and began to dream he had died and was a wandering soul in an alien world. Dreamwalking, he thought about the universe and its infinitude of stars and dimensions and he thought with supreme longing of his exwife and with regret of all the harshness that never should have been between them and how in another possible dimension they were happy together at this moment and he was in bed with her at this moment and her smooth bloodwarm woman's skin was absorbing his pain at this moment and then he thought of all the black space in the universe and all that loneliness and the lost souls like him plodding within its endlessness and he thought of his pains comparatively, the one inside or those collected on the outside and which the worse was, and those of the past and those of now, and he kept walking, the planet turning under his feet as he walked, and he thought of the mass dead hanging like spoiled fruit in the trees in the green hills by the river that whispered in burbles like ashen sprits to the living and who they had been and who they had loved and why they had died and then he tried to quiet his mind but could not could not.

Pinto

THE
BUTCHER,
THE
BAKER

TERRY WRIGHT

S HE HAD RUN the bakers out of their minds. An official video of the gallows was shot on phone and cut up for cookbooks. Blood mixed well with the batter. The recipe's neck was broken, and audible cracks reached agreement in the oven. Every bag fell through a trap and was listened to with a stethoscope, but Nestle's lawyers still found loopholes. Ruth Wakefield said genocide was medieval. She received a lifetime supply of rebukes and shouts. Older editions of her Toll House were occupied by multinational forces and food lecturers. A nightclub in Tikrit suspended her desserts. The prisoner asked a witness if he heard the mixer's vibrations. As he approached the platform, he struggled and assumed it would melt. But home-cooked meals at Camp Justice were softened to retain a creamy texture, and care packages from movie stars did not tremble. It's normal for militants to serve ruined dough and a semisweet noose. This is not how things really happen. Buttered up on hard audio, he held his shape. His cookies were handed a red card as concoctions burned on the outskirts. War crimes treats for everyone. Soon, hundreds of GIs were writing home and asking their families to send them some.

Java

A
DEATH
IN
CUSTODY

CHLOE HOOPER

Palm Island, off the coast of Far North Queensland, was settled in 1918 as a reserve for "troublesome blacks." With a population of 2,500 people, it is now one of the largest Aboriginal communities in Australia. Chloe Hooper's piece on Palm Island's first jailhouse death ever to lead to charges against a police officer appeared last year, in McSweeney's *21; this is an account of what's happened since then.*

O N THE MORNING of November 19, 2004, Senior Sergeant Chris Hurley, Palm Island's rangy thirty-three-year-old officer in charge, had arrested Cameron Doomadgee, thirty-six, for committing a public nuisance. Doomadgee was drunk—"happy drunk," community members said—and singing his favorite song, "Who Let the Dogs Out?" But Hurley heard him swear and locked him in the police van. There was a struggle when they arrived at the watch house, and Doomadgee punched Hurley in the jaw. Within forty-five minutes of his arrest, Cameron Doomadgee was dead, with a black eye, a liver almost cleaved in two, four broken ribs, a ruptured portal vein, and a hemorrhaging pancreas. Senior Sergeant Hurley claimed that Doomadgee had tripped and fallen over a step.

In video recordings of Cameron Doomadgee's funeral, hundreds of Palm Islanders walk with his coffin on the narrow road from the island's Catholic church to the cemetery. The journey is several kilometers and the sun blisteringly hot. At the front of the procession is Doomadgee's fifteen-year-old son, Eric, small for his age, holding a white wooden cross to place on his father's grave.

Eric Doomadgee now has his own white cross. Last July, Cameron's only child was found hanging from a tree in bushland on Palm Island. The family friends who found him cut his body down and carried it into town.

On the morning of Eric's funeral, his body was laid out in a small outbuilding of the hospital. People lined up in single file to pay their respects. Eric's friends, Palm Island's young men, had dressed in long-sleeved maroon shirts and black trousers. Others wore maroon, yellow, or white: the colors of his favorite rugby team, the Brisbane Broncos. His cousins had ribbons in these colors pinned to their clothes.

Inside the building there started a terrible keening. Slowly, the line moved past Eric in the coffin, white silk around his neck. People touched his face and hair. In front of him sat his mother and his aunts and his stepmother, Tracy, all of them weeping. Grief had taken them somewhere far away. From the time he was a toddler, Eric had been passed constantly between households. Two of Eric's aunts, Elizabeth and Claudelle, had even breastfed him after his own mother, who had a drinking problem, left him.

As the hearse drove to the church, people stood outside their houses, bowing their heads. Drivers pulled their cars over and did the same. Inside the overflowing church, plastic flowers were attached with masking tape to each pew. Mourners also stood outside, staring in through the cyclone-wire windows. "Jesus said, 'Let not your heart be troubled,'" the black preacher announced. She did not address the circumstances of Eric's life, or why he might have ended it, nor his father's life and why it might have ended. The sermon felt perfunctory: apparently, recognizing Jesus as the Way, the Truth, and the Life could ease a troubled mind.

Colin Tatz, a social scientist and historian, has written at length on Australian Aboriginal youth suicide, which may be as much as 40 percent higher than in Australia's nonindigenous population. Although he warns of the impossibility of ever truly understanding why someone has ended their life, he has created an indigenous "typology." There is the *existential suicide,* the person who "sees no horizon and... no means of altering such horizons as they have." Driving with an elder one day, I saw a group of youths in the hip-hop clothes of Black America, shoulders hunched: *I will fail.* The elder said, "Who knows the potential of these young men?" On the island, to reach puberty is to reach the abyss. The young inherit a community with 92 percent unemployment, where half the men are dead by fifty, where they own nothing, control nothing, have sovereignty over nothing but their own bodies.

Then there is the *grieving suicide,* the person trapped in the cycle of mourning dead friends and relatives. On Palm Island, people are still mourning one death when the next occurs: one woman told me that she went to three relatives' funerals in two weeks; another said that she went to her mother's and sister's funerals on the same day. Outside the church, blank-faced women carried hand towels in case they had to wipe their eyes. Young men stood very still, crying. None of Eric's friends would consider counseling, just as he hadn't after his father died.

Eric's cousins told me he wanted justice for his father and was making a stand. The *political suicide,* according to Tatz, occurs when the young person has a score to settle, particularly with the police: "It is both a rebuke and a stand against authority." In North Queensland's indigenous communities, hanging carries particular nuances, including "martyrdom, pathos, capital punishment, the legal system, and injustice." In 1989 there was a Royal Commission into Aboriginal Deaths in Custody, exploring why so many blacks die in jail. Since then, committing suicide in custody has come to be understood as "a powerful symbolic statement of oppression and injustice." Eric might have been communing with the dead. There can be camaraderie, intimacy, solidarity in imitating someone else's death. Had he in some way gestured toward the way his father died?

The Palm Island cemetery is a field of white wooden crosses. Most graves are carefully tended and adorned with colorful plastic flowers. Eric's friends had jostled so intensely to be pallbearers— from "Church to hearse," from "Turnoff to last coconut tree," from "Last coconut tree to gravesite"—that the coffin almost broke. They passed around a shovel to fill the grave, covering the coffin swathed in maroon, yellow, and white flowers.

After the burial, the young men all posed for photographs in front of the grave. They had a group shot, then took turns having single shots taken. They crouched close to the newly formed mound, touching it tenderly. There was something reminiscent of young Palestinians posing for the video camera before blowing themselves up.

The family waited patiently for Eric's friends to finish, then they too stood in front of the grave. There were separate shots of Eric's aunts, cousins, and even the in-laws, the husbands and wives of Eric's cousins. "Smile! Smile!" called Dwayne, Eric's retarded cousin. It was the photographer, he thought, who was meant to smile.

Four days after Eric's funeral, the inquest into his father's death sat for the last time. All evidence had been taken and the lawyers were making their final submissions. The family had made the three-hour boat ride from Palm Island to Townsville—the regional center of North Queensland. On the street outside the courthouse, Elizabeth Doomadgee, one of Cameron's sisters, ran into two boys who were returning to their family on Palm Island. One had been in foster care with a white family, and had been beaten. Elizabeth told them that they would be welcome to stay at her house whenever they wanted, but there were two rules. "One: If you go out somewhere, if you go fishing or something, you tell someone. Two: Church on Sundays." She told me later that her house was always open to little children. She might have been thinking of Eric. With her youngest child now in high school, she cares for four foster children under ten years old.

Walking into the inquest, Elizabeth said, "A mustard seed can move a mountain." She was thinking of Matthew 17:20—"If ye have faith as a grain of mustard seed, ye shall say unto this mountain, Remove hence to yonder place; and it shall remove." The inquest was a mountain of legal precedent and sections and codes, of closed-rank police and rival personalities along the bar table, of one-upmanship, adrenaline and ego. The mountain is the legal game.

Then Tracy Twaddle walked to the witness box. Her face had the same fine features as the Doomadgee women: bobbed hair, bow-lips. Her large body was hunched in old clothes, in widow's black with a print of white flowers. She kept her eyes down. Last year, she'd gone to the hospital with pneumonia after sleeping at night on Cameron's grave. In a soft voice, she read out a statement. A lot of people cried. She said her piece modestly, without a hint of guile:

"I met Cameron in 1994 and we lived together soon after that. We had a simple but happy life together. He was unselfish, and he was caring, and he tried to do the right thing by the people. He'd help anybody. He didn't—he didn't care what color they were. He wasn't mean. He was always caring. He was always there for me and his mum and his family.

"And Cameron was always joking and ready for a laugh, you know, he always lifted our spirits. I think he saw the good and right in life. And he never sat around and brooded over things.

And in a way he was an inspiration to me, because I used to watch him and, you know, think Gee, he knew how to enjoy his life. He was content. It was a simple life and happy.

"Cameron was a hunter and he was proud to carry on that tradition. He was a proud hunter. He was always proud that he could provide food for us—goat, possum, fish—and share it out amongst his family and friends.

"Cameron was, you know, more or less in his prime when this happened to him—when he lost his life. He was still a young man, and he had a lot to look forward to. He was especially proud of his son, Eric—he meant the world to Cameron. He was a proud father, and to watch his son grow and to be there when Eric became a man was something Cameron always talked about, but that's never going to happen now.

"My life is on hold. I get frustrated because everything's dragging on slowly. I think about if we're ever going to get real justice for him.

"Eric was even more in a state of anguish than I was and tragically Eric killed himself just a couple of weeks ago. In spite of this, you know, I'll always try to be positive, because of Cameron. He's never far from my mind. That's all I can say."

In the course of the inquest, lawyers for Queensland's Police Commissioner and Hurley twice tried to prevent the Senior Sergeant's prior complaint files from being seen by the other lawyers and used in evidence. Their applications to the Supreme Court failed, and also slowed the inquest so that an enormous amount of evidence *was* amassed. More than a dozen police were directed to appear, but they had seen no evil, heard no evil, and would certainly not be speaking of any evil. The inquest also heard from two Aboriginal men who claimed that Hurley had assaulted them during arrests for minor offenses. Hurley denied both allegations. The most unfortunate testimony regarding a prior incident, however, came from Barbara Pilot. A Palm Island woman in her thirties, Pilot happens to be the daughter of Cameron Doomadgee's eldest sister.

On the night of May 19, 2004, Pilot and her partner, Arthur Murray, were drunk. Murray pushed her down some stairs and hit her in the back of the head with a screwdriver. While an ambulance took Pilot to the hospital, Senior Sergeant Hurley arrived to perform his usual thankless task. He arrested Murray and put him in the back of the van. As he was driving away, Pilot returned. She approached the van, remonstrating with Hurley, who told her to go away. When she did not, she claims, he reversed over her bare foot. "She made the exclamation that I'd run her over," Hurley said. "She was singing it out. I can't recall whether she was screaming in pain but she was singing out, 'You run me over!'" It was dark, but Hurley opened the door and looked Pilot up and down. Seeing no injuries, he drove away. Pilot arrived back at the hospital with, the attending doctor said, "the bone clearly protruding from her foot in a very unusual manner."

A bone specialist from Townsville, where Pilot needed surgery, and a forensic pathologist on retainer from Hurley's lawyers, also told the inquest that Pilot's injuries were consistent with her having been run over. In fact, even Hurley admitted the possibility: "I'd be ignorant to do that; to exclude it 100 percent."

But the night it happened, that is exactly what he tried to do. He called his superior and family friend, Inspector Gary Hickey, to report the incident. At the inquest, Hickey read from a bound book the notes he'd taken of the conversation: "'More consistent with kicking ground but possibly from car... Hurley claims not possible from position near driver's window.'" Then, of the victim: "'Intoxicated, playing up.'" Hickey ordered Hurley to start investigating the incident.

This relatively minor episode is like the Rosetta stone of the death in custody, decoding a model of police recalcitrance. The Senior Sergeant invents an alternative story: she was kicking the ground. (Or, he tripped over a step.) He gets involved in the investigation himself. Then, his supporters step in. In June 2004, Warren Webber, who later headed the investigation into Doomadgee's death, commissioned Hurley's close friend Detective Darren Robinson, who also investigated Doomadgee's death, to look into Pilot's complaint. Robinson waited a month before he began. By this time, her foot had healed. Robinson did not speak to any of her doctors, or even to Pilot herself; instead he reported to his superiors that her claims were "fictitious."

Late last September, Queensland's Deputy State Coroner, Christine Clements, handed down her findings from the eighteen-month inquest into the death of Cameron Doomadgee. That morning at the Townsville Court House, four armed police officers stood outside the small courtroom, and one armed officer waited inside with a gun, pepper spray, handcuffs: the full utility belt. Many Palm Islanders had traveled to Townsville to hear the findings, but there was only seating for twenty. They were not feeling optimistic.

Far North Queensland is Australia's "Deep North": in the early twentieth century tribes of Aborigines were still being "dispersed" by raiding parties that often included the local constabulary, who cut notches into the stocks of their rifles. One hundred years later, frontier attitudes may not be so different. Last year, a market-research firm conducted a poll to establish a statistical profile of the Townsville community. More than four hundred people were asked about their perceptions of Aboriginals in North Queensland. Nearly half the responses were "negative themed": "They are mongrel dogs"; "They drink too much and they smell"; "I don't have an opinion except to shoot them all."

The Deputy Coroner, an attractive, inscrutable woman in her mid-forties, quoted from the Royal Commission into Aboriginal Deaths in Custody: "'A death in custody is a public matter. Police and prison officers perform their services on behalf of the community. They must be accountable for the proper performance of their duties. Justice requires that both the individual interest of the deceased's family and the general interest of the community be served by the conduct of thorough, competent, and impartial investigations into all deaths in custody.'"

The investigation into Doomadgee's death, Clements said,

"failed to meet those standards." She found that it was "unwise and inappropriate" for Hurley to be investigated by his friends, and for Hurley to pick up these investigators from the airport and drive them around; that it was "a serious error of judgement" for the investigators to share a meal with Hurley at his home that evening; that the investigation was "compromised" by Hurley having the chance to discuss the investigation with other witnesses; and that it was "reprehensible" that no allegation of assault was provided to the pathologist. The senior investigating officers, Clements said, were "willfully blind."

Witnesses claimed that from outside the police station they had heard Doomadgee crying for help as he lay writhing in pain on the cell floor. The Deputy Coroner concluded that at least one of these cries must have been heard by Hurley, and that his response was "totally inadequate."

Senior Sergeant Hurley has maintained that Doomadgee died as a result of tripping and falling over a step. After a fact-finding mission costing millions of dollars, the Deputy Coroner did not find this version of events credible: "The consensus of expert medical opinion was that a simple fall through the doorway, even in an uncontrolled and accelerated fashion, was unlikely to have caused the particular injury."

Her voice was quavering as she read out the last pages: "Despite a steady demeanour in court, Senior Sergeant Hurley's explanation does not persuade me he was truthful in his account of what happened. I find that Senior Sergeant Hurley hit Mulrunji [Doomadgee's tribal name] whilst he was on the floor a number of times in direct response to himself having been hit in the jaw and then falling to the floor… This is consistent with the medical evidence of the injuries that caused Mulrunji's death… I conclude that these actions of Senior Sergeant Hurley caused the fatal injuries.'"

The courtroom took a deep collective breath. The Doomadgees all burst into tears. The police lawyers shook their heads.

That afternoon, the president of the Queensland Police Union, Gary Wilkinson, went on the attack. A burly, red-faced man, he appeared on television full of righteous outrage: "Senior Sergeant Hurley has been hung out to dry," he said. The Deputy Coroner had "conducted a witch hunt from the start that's been designed to pander to the residents of Palm Island, rather than establishing the facts. Clearly she approached this inquest as a foregone conclusion despite the mountain of evidence in support of Chris Hurley that she deliberately overlooked."

Just what the mountain of evidence comprised, no one knew; but the following invitation soon appeared on the Queensland Police Union's website:

> Send you [*sic*] support to Chris Hurley—click here
> All messages of support are appericated [*sic*] and will be
> passed onto Senior Sergeant Hurley.
> supportchris@qpu.asn.au.

"All of us know only too well," claims the Police Union, "that what happened to Chris Hurley could happen to any one of us."

* * *

Early this year, Senior Sergeant Hurley was charged with man-slaughter; he became the first police officer in Australia ever to have been tried for an Aboriginal death in custody.

In late June, after a six-day trial, he was acquitted. The all-white jury found it plausible that Cameron Doomadgee's injuries were, in fact, due to a "complicated fall" over a step. Almost immediately, the police union released a series of radio advertisements attacking the Queensland government for having allowed the trial to go forward. The Doomadgee family is now preparing for a civil suit; Senior Sergeant Hurley is still on the job.

Persian Arab

what

NO
EMPRESS
EYES

Padgett Powell

No Empress Eyes In Here had first been named No Empress, then No Empress Eyes, and then the owner's daughter, hearing the name but not knowing it applied to a horse, said, "No empress eyes in *here,*" and the final name was set. She was ten years old, the daughter. Then they told her that No Empress Eyes In Here disappeared during the Kentucky Derby when she fell through a trapdoor in the track. She went down a laundry chute not to China but to some other inscrutable place no one knew anything about or where it was, so "She might as well," the daughter said, "have gone to China," for all they could do about it. Thereafter the horse was known as No Empress Eyes Down There.

At the same time there was a boy in Kansas, also ten, who dreamed of inventing a new kind of combine that would not harm animals when it came upon them in the wheat. Specifically the boy was thinking about fawns, who were told by their mothers, who had galloped away, to stay put no matter what, and who, the fawns, would stay put no matter what, no matter if a combine with a twenty-four-foot-wide worm blade came upon them and scooped them up and sprayed them into the wheat in pieces no larger than the wheat. This very much bothered the boy, who wanted to be a farmer badly except for this one thing, turning baby deer into bloody wheat. So he wanted a humane combine. He thought and thought and could not come up with an idea for a combine that would pick up the deer and set it to the side and pet it and send it trotting off to the place its mother had hightailed it to after abandoning it in the field with the diesel monster bearing down on it. He wanted the combine to issue citations for negligent parenting too, paste them gently to the fawns before they trotted off to their mothers, or the combine might call the department of human resources and have them take the fawn away from the mother as it did children from human parents who did things not nearly as bad as leave their children in the tall grass in front of huge machines, but he would never invent a machine that would do all this, that was very fantastic thinking, he wanted a real machine to really rescue the fawns, forget about justice. He thought and thought and finally arrived at a compromise suggested by the man at the Brandt's meat market in Lucas: the fawn could be scooped up and blown whole into another chamber, probably dead, but not in a million pieces. Okay, the boy said, okay.

Until he could invent the new combine he drove the conventional combine so slowly that everyone was unpleased with him during harvest but he did not care. He was through with scooping up fawns. He was disgusted with these people, like John

Deere, who probably called themselves that for a joke, and a joke about killing deer was not funny. They had a slogan, "Runs like a Deere"; it ought to be "Runs *down* a Deere."

After the horse she'd named fell through the track and no one did anything about it, the horse owner's daughter felt she'd had it with these people and ran away. It went well for a while, was not too frightening when she was on the bus, but then she was walking a long way and in the country and she hid in a field, and a giant machine came up on her with a big steel like barber-pole thing turning and cutting the grass. It stopped, the machine, coming at her, but the barber pole did not stop turning and hissing, and a boy got out of the glass cabin on top of the machine and blaring music came out with him, like Queen, or Aerosmith, and she wondered what kind of hicks they had out here wherever she was. "Well," the boy said, "do you want to run like a deer or be run *down* like a deer?" That was about the coolest thing she had ever heard anyone say whether he was a hick or not and she got in the cabin and they mowed some more field.

Then they went to his cave. It was in the side of a creek bank with no water in the creek and it was filled with a lot of appliances that did not work because there was no power. He had floor lamps in it with fringe on the shades, and a big kitchen stove, and an old TV with a wood cabinet that looked like an aquarium full of dull green algae and no fish, and a brass bed that was brown from the moisture in the cave. There were no bats. The boy said he wanted bats but none ever came in that he saw. There were only dried-up roots hanging from the ceiling. These felt like bats when you touched them. If it were her cave she would trim the ceiling, the horse owner's daughter thought.

They decided they had to tell someone where she was but the boy was afraid he would be arrested for kidnapping and molesting her. "All you did was run me down like a deer," the girl said, suddenly wondering what became of the jockey on her horse that had gone down the hole in the track. Really, nothing had been said at all about the jockey; it was a thoroughly unsatisfying business, that horse disappearing, and horse-racing in general, and now here was a boy talking about molesting her who had not so much as touched her, he had no idea what molesting even meant. She didn't either. "Why don't you molest me then?" she said.

"Good idea, since I will be arrested for it." The boy threw himself on the moldy bed. "I don't know what *molest* means, actually."

"I don't either. Whatever it is, don't do it."

"Okay. I won't." The boy had crossed his feet and put his hands behind his head. "*Man,*" he said, "this is like *living!*"

They both envisioned living in the cave for a good long time away from horrible and boring horse-racing and horrible and boring farming—"But farming is not boring, just horrible, and just the fawn grinding," the boy said—but they knew they couldn't make it very long in a cave. "That is *fant*asy thinking," the boy said.

"No Empress Eyes Down Here," the girl said, and the boy did not ask what in the world was she talking about. He just got out of bed and adjusted his pliers on his belt and said, "Come on." He was very cool, in her judgment. They held hands crossing the field.

"I think holding hands is part of molesting," the girl said.

"Okay," the boy said. "I will be ar*rest*ed." He clearly enjoyed saying *arrested*.

At the farm the boy's father called the Sheriff and reported having the girl with no more travail than he might have reported the wheat to be too wet to harvest, and his mother set a place at the table almost as if they had expected her and certainly as if she were a guest they were pleased to have and not a runaway with legal strings attached to her. If anyone was going to be arrested it was not going to be them, or even her, it seemed. The mother told her everything would be fine and she could plan to stay with them until they heard from the Sheriff.

"We want to live a long time together in the cave," the boy said.

"We'll have to run some Romex out there after dinner," the boy's father said, "in that case." He was eating and perhaps joking, you could not get a good look at his mouth for the food going in. He had on his belt the same kind of pliers the boy had on his. He wore jeans and nonpointy boots and no hat. These Kansas people were not like Texas people, the Texas people she had met in New Jersey. The girl had had enough of Texas people with their ridiculous boots and jewelry, always scaring the horses and trying to buy everything in sight. She had not seen a Kansas person try to buy anything and she had not heard one be loud.

This was more like it. If they were going to run Romex to the cave, whatever that meant, she would help them.

The food was odd. "What's the name of this again?" she asked, about some balls of something like pancake they were eating in syrup. "Evilskeever," the woman said. "And this?" The girl took a bite of another food they'd served her to show she was not critical of it. It was also in a ball, but a mushy and not a cakey one. "Ham-and-bean glob," the boy said. "It's the best." There was no salt and pepper in sight. Everything was served in a bland ball. These people had figured a few things out. At her house eating was a trial, a series of repellent exotic challenges, everything so seasoned that it stank. Out here you could relax and eat, it looked like, without worrying about it.

She had learned too that they had a horse—*one,* a working horse, named Carl. After this dinner of pancake balls and ham-and-bean mushballs they could put Romex on Carl and get her a little set of pliers for her own belt and head for the cave, and with her pliers she was going to tear out those roots coming out of the ceiling as her contribution to all the sense-making going on out here in the middle of nowhere. A horse was not going to disappear out here. They could listen to Aerosmith or Queen or Genesis if they wanted to. She hoped the Sheriff was corrupt or lazy or incompetent and did not call her father. Really, if a horse disappeared out here, there would be some answers for it, some answering for someone to do. Carl did not disappear or do anything else ridiculous, he did his job and ate his feed and waited for his next job, which did not involve being skittish and violent and lame and sick and costing everyone so much money and anxiety that they got divorces and heart attacks. What they needed back in New Jersey was a horse named Carl and some ham-and-bean glob to settle their nerves. She was not going back if she could help it. "Man," she said suddenly, and everyone looked at her, "this is living!" They laughed.

"I need some of those pliers," she said.

"No problem," the father said, between gooey evilskeevers, of which he had eaten eighteen by her count. He was outright hoovering the evilskeevers. Another good sign.

Outside in the dusk the boy picked up a piece of bailing wire and wound it loosely around her finger. He pulled out his pliers in a motion so quick that she wanted pliers all the more and he twisted the bailing wire lightly until it snugged on her finger and then he clipped the twist close, leaving a loose ring of galvanized wire on her finger and them both appraising it. "You are my wife," the boy said. "Okay?"

"Sure," the girl said. "Sure." She fingered the sharp little nub of the clipped twist and made the ring travel around her finger. The father approached with a set of pliers and a small leather holster that looked old and oily and forgotten until now, and they put it on her belt.

They went fishing in their pond and the girl caught two catfish and the men caught nothing. With her own pliers the girl removed the hook from her catfish, the first fish she had ever caught. Seeing this, the boy said, "You have to bait your own hook too. If you don't, you will be arrested." At dark they went home. The kitchen was cleaned of all evidence of evilskeever and ham-and-bean glob, and the Sheriff had not called, and they went to bed. This was living.

CONTRIBUTORS

EMILY ANDERSON's fiction and poetry have appeared in the *Denver Quarterly, Caketrain, Indelible Kitchen,* and *Bailliwik.* Her performances and videos have appeared at numerous venues, including Chicago's Museum of Contemporary Art, Prop Thtr, Roots & Culture, Heir Gallery, and the Gene Siskel Film Center. She lives in Madrid.

KENNETH BONERT's short story "Packers and Movers" was shortlisted for the Journey Prize. He lives in Toronto.

DAVID HOLLANDER is the author of the novel *L.I.E.,* and has published fiction and nonfiction in *Swink,* the *New York Times Magazine, Unsaid,* and *Poets & Writers.*

CHLOE HOOPER's first novel, *A Child's Book of True Crime,* was shortlisted for the Orange Prize. She is working on a book about the Palm Island death, to be published by Scribner.

CONNOR KILPATRICK is a native Texan. He lives in New York. "Yuri" is his first published story.

ALEXANDER MACBRIDE is a linguist who lives in Los Angeles.

STEVEN MILLHAUSER's fourth collection of stories, *Dangerous Laughter,* is due out next spring. His other books include *The*

Knife Thrower, Martin Dressler, and *Edwin Mullhouse: The Life and Death of an American Writer.* He lives in Saratoga Springs, New York.

PADGETT POWELL has written six books of fiction and teaches that which cannot be taught at the University of Florida.

JOYCE CAROL OATES's most recent novel is *The Gravedigger's Daughter.* She teaches at Princeton.

TERRY WRIGHT is the author of five books/chapbooks of poetry. He teaches creative writing at the University of Central Arkansas. He is also a digital artist. See for yourself at http://wrightart.net.

ABOUT THE ARTISTS

AMY JEAN PORTER's continuing "Tiny Horses Say What" series aims to encompass more than two hundred of the world's horse breeds. Her other projects include "Birds of North America Misquote Hip-Hop and Sometimes Pause for Reflection" (508 drawings) and "North American Mammals Speak the Truth and Often Flatter You Unnecessarily" (319 drawings).

LEAH HAYES draws in ball-point pen and records music under the name Scary Mansion. Her book, *Holy Moly,* is out from Fantagraphics, and her illustrations have appeared in the *New York Times* and *Punk Planet* (RIP).

Italian Heavy Draft